Shadows That Speak

GITTE TAMAR

BTW LLC

To those who have never been called weird.
I pity you for you have yet to live a life with no fear.

Acknowledgment

I token my family for supporting the oddity of dreams that have shaped me into the individual I was truly meant to be.

Rather than forcing me into the societal box of boring redundancy my parents, Kimberly and Craig encouraged each of my unique attributes. When called into parent-teacher conferences as a child to discuss my gravitation towards tones of darker narratives my parents commended my creativity by surprising me with bedtime stories from Edgar Allen Poe and for that, I will forever be grateful.

To my Brother, Dominic, thank you for dealing with my shenanigans.

To my dearest Nan, Sharon, thank you for your continual love and the ability to always shake things up.

To my wonderful dogs, Stella and Mrs. Darcy, thank you for keeping me sane.

Contents

One

FATHER, IS THAT YOU?

1875, England

It was a forgotten night. Cold gusts of air curled across the pavement as if summoned to pass by. Did you know the wind is soulless? Yes, think about it. Airy currents flow past people and disappear in the flicker of an eye. The wind waltzes past...leaving no trace other than a pathway cleared of rubbish and stench. Like the breeze, I too am cleansing. I have no reason to disguise my acts, for they are just and enlightened.

My honesty about the ensuing events remains without suspect. Any modifications to the accounts I am about to reveal to you are lies. My existence is like the wind; our similarities entice the breeze to accompany me like a lost puppy searching for its mother. I appear serene, but looks can deceive, for I enjoy wreaking destruction and basking in the tones of chiming screams and cherish a twist of uncertainty.

Some claim I am evil. Evil? Ha! I howl at their naivete. Who's afraid of the Big Bad Wolf...a coward, that's who! Through living, I have discovered that to satisfy humanity's perspective regarding evil, you must be vile. Under society's judgmental eye, evil is unkempt, smelling of piss, poverty-stricken; being handsome and rich automatically excludes me from the title of "evil." I am merely a darkened spirit that dwells within this statuesque frame. I know how to live and recognize what drives my contentment. I appreciate the murkier aspects of existence, possess a secret fancy for justice, and enjoy grasping what others dare not take. Do you understand? Imagine seizing the warmth from the depth of a person's being. The mere prospect of it provides me the craving to endure. By embodying the hunter in a macabre tale, I reclaim my youth. Paradoxically, the predatory act makes me even more alluring to women.

I've determined what I loathe most about women is their wealth-seeking mentality. They are amusing creatures--most only marry for materialistic reasons, such as social escalation or financial gain. If I were ugly as a bear with overfilled pockets, a well-suited woman would gladly marry me. I can have any female of my choosing! Do you consider me arrogant? Typically, one would give themselves the benefit of the doubt, but I am an honorable fellow, as well as the most narcissistic being you will ever meet.

My confidence is justified. I am young, attractive, and affluent as hell. Everything about me is superb, including my collection. "What assemblage?" you may ask. Why, the store of victims I have tossed onto my trophy shelves throughout the years. One might expect I'm teasing, but in fact, it is not a theoretical collection. Being modest, I will not divulge all the boring details of my altruistic purge of rubbish from the world, although I will share what I believe to be most paramount.

My method of carrying out my life's purpose is flawless. Touring from place to place, I have no acquaintances, and like the wind, I am out of people's lives before they can lay any accusations. Some might speculate as to how I select which market animals to pluck from humanity and the details behind my justification. Now, before you cringe with revulsion, I only choose those who exhibit qualities like mine: they must be vain and possess an undying hunger for affluence.

As a youthful suitor who reads the age of thirty, stands tall and is rather stylish, I have few problems accessing the cattle I choose to harvest. I am not impolite for branding the name of "cattle" onto the enticing creatures, for they too have owners, often referred to as "parents," who, without hesitancy, will auction them off to men who offer the loftiest social positions. When cultivated the societal way, these women become ruined, and I must rid humanity of such monstrosities. They are worthless, lowly specimens whose eradication we will not lament. Like a domino trampling the next, they too obliterate those who stand in the way of their rapacious appetites.

Before you judge my existence, please look at your own. *We are animals.* We have developed from beasts; therefore, we are inclined to hunt like beasts. I have learned to welcome what I am.

Picture a flower forming from a bud. It first appears insignificant; then, over time, warm soothing air blows life into its succulent veins, filling the helpless budding babe with life. Society has destined this beautiful image for cruelty. Think about it: why nurture the flower, knowing that once it burgeons, it will be hacked down, slashed from its youth! Lifeblood will never invade the bloom's veins again. Civilization's careless disregard of life's beauty is archaic and thoughtless. A flower has done no wrong, but society has determined its sole purpose is to function as a simple decoration. I am that flower, cut down and cast aside by society at too young an age.

Some might have referred to me as an orphan, but the term is too charming; "scum" is more befitting. My value was nothing more than that of an infinitesimal insect no one cared if they trod upon. Like the blossom, I assumed my life would end prematurely. I would lie on the streets at night, wishing for someone to put me out of my misery, exterminate me from a rotten world that wouldn't allow me a fighting chance. Frequently I prayed for death, but no one answered my pleas.

Do not grieve for me, for through my anguish a glimpse of intrigue entered my life--some might even suggest a guardian angel. On one especially unsympathetic night, from an alley's feces- and rat-infested corner emanated a voice so quiet that the words might pass unnoticed if one were not attentive. The brusque voice presented as a whisper so intoxicating that it drew me to stare at the corner in a trancelike state. My breath hung on every word as I listened to the melodic verbiage repeat over the course of several nights. No one dared invade the pitch-black corner, for whenever someone had tried, they didn't emerge the same. The intolerable stench made my eyes water and ache with tears, yet I overlooked it to determine who was behind the voice that consoled me. The tone was bewitching. Even if I were hallucinating, I was at an age where I ached for an ardent figure to bolster me. I dare say I loved this shadowy voice that soothed me.

Though a name or gender was never divulged, I decided it was a masculine figure based on the timbre of his voice. Therefore, from this moment forward, I will refer to the voice as "he." He never offered me his name, nor did I ever know his character. Deep down, I recognized he was the only one who gave two shits about me and my sorrowful existence. The voice assured me refinement and prosperity, which at that moment was all I craved. I needed to show the world I am someone you should give two shits about. I am almighty.

The initial tasks assigned to me by the enigmatic voice started as petty misdeeds, such as stealing. He wished the best for me and knew I needed money to survive. Well, hell, we are past the point of giving him the meaningless title of "he." From now on, I will refer to him as "Father." Yes, Father! Reared up as a bastard child with no fatherly example to study, I found this title was the most fitting. As I became closer to Father, I desensitized myself to the hostile world. The only beings in existence were Father and me, and together we would transform humanity.

As the streets filled with darkness, I retreated to my cobblestone alley, where I found comfort with Father. The cold stones lay still under my feet, darkness oozing from their veinlike fractures. The night stood quiet as the sky conjured up an unusual turn of events. A shift, as momentous as the earth leaping, was about to begin.

Curled up in the shadowy corner, frozen from the bitter cold, I sensed a comforting spectral blanket had been flung over me, separating me from my murky surroundings. The consolatory action was the closest I have been to experiencing love. Encased in Father's presence, I heard his tender whisper, which only I could decipher. He advised me I must be brave to flourish. Considering his intentions to be authentic, I freed my ears to attend to the wisdom that flowed from his mouth.

From his guidance, I recognized the spiny backbone of civilization to be women. Women's values are tainted by their environment, picking up from their parents to seek prosperity above all else, including love. Little did I realize an extraordinary calling to purge humanity of these ruined creatures was about to be slung upon my soul. Father instructed me not to consider the spoiled ones as human but as cattle, for they had proved their authentic existence and provided no other benefit to society than slaughter. As I stared into the blackness, I pledged to comply with his wishes, for he was the only one who ever cared for me.

With the money I had collected foraging from undeserving pockets, I bought suitable clothes to woo the most selective of women. Father recommended I rehearse before committing to reform the world. At his directive, I frequented high-class bordellos with the initial intent of honing my social and sexual prowess. The nights grew darker when I went out to play. Brothels thirstily opened their gates, anticipating my glorious arrival. To breach the chambers, you must embody the part. Without Father luring each heavy pocket filled with coins to fuel my expenditures, I would not have secured admittance.

As I strode through the shadowiness of the ever-familiar cobblestone pavement, a blackness deluged my spirit, and for a moment I thought I was drowning. I considered whether to combat the darkness, but it was marvelous, my stride becoming bolder with every step. Fear was no longer a virtue but a lusting; I craved to see others' dread. All my life, I had feared the world around me and the horrors it excreted upon me. With my new stability, however, the tables had shifted.

In the distance, I smelled a familiar rot basking in the air. These were my people, my kin. All heartbeats on earth grew louder as each approaching minute elevated my anticipation. The vibration grew so loud that my thoughts and speech no longer had room to exist. Once again, Father's presence filled my carcass with stability. At last, I arrived at the fated brothel door.

Who built this wretched dungeon entry? Its contents reeked of heartless souls appealing for anyone to break their existence of immoral standing. As I pounded on the impenetrable devil's gate, a surge of anxiety coursed through me. The door inched open with the utmost of caution, revealing a fellow of considerable stature. He almost looked heroic as he stood robed in all black. Gold accents embellished his red and gray coattails, which trailed like flags, welcoming my arrival. His impeccably slicked mane was black as midnight, with silver adorning his temples. It was clear that he had the assets to entice any female who captured his attention. Maybe that's how he started his shop. Like Satan himself, he persuaded the most beguiling members of society to serve in his brothel. Now, seeing him in all his illustriousness as he stood at the entrance, I was beside myself. I called it a brothel, but it was much more luxurious than that. The man hosted a dainty-- yes, dainty--establishment. As I continued looking at him, I swore he became taller with the anticipation of the words that would flow from my tongue. With self-assurance, I looked him square in the eyes and declared, "I understand you have the finest, and I very much fancy some company tonight." I clattered the coins in my pocket while alluding to an inheritance. He studied me up and down, fixing his sight on my jewel-encrusted pocket watch; without a second thought, he summoned me in.

He glanced both ways down the desolate street and slammed the devilish door behind me, sealing me inside. I swore the hinges chuckled about the deception that was about to befall this "master of a man." He led me into a chamber that had an atrocious color scheme of putrid mustard yellow. Then, one by one, he brought out the cattle from behind a beckoning red curtain. They were physically beautiful; one may only speculate how they had given in to such treachery. Their souls, once full of purity, had been snatched from their bodies for a few shillings. Within moments, a dozen young women stood before me. Unlike what you might expect, they looked dignified, clad in ceremonious attire. From left to right, I scanned down the line, questioning which victim to select. At the end of the row of faces, a wench caught my view. She scanned the livestock to her left with a competitive and appallingly smug grin and, like clockwork, leaned over just enough to supply me a quick glimpse of what she offered. Hunger seared in her eyes, and a need for attention oozed from her veins. It was as if she were bleeding out all of society's deepest desires. To get a better view, I swept back my black locks to uncover my golden eyes. As my manicured, well-boned finger rose to summon her, it was sickening how proud she appeared at having been selected. Her eyes lit up as she taunted the other females who surrounded her, carrying on as if she had won first prize at a fair. She was mistaken.

It was not a trophy she had gained but a one-way ticket to hell.

Soon she would visit the very depths of damnation, to which she had already sold her soul. Do not pity her, for she would hastily reach her ambitions. All the other cattle vanished as the rotten one continued to make it known that she had earned my attention. As she approached, I noticed her pupils glowed red with loathing. She was the spawn of Lucifer himself. The proprietor showed us down a corridor to a set of stairs. After we ascended the staircase, he pointed to an impressive door and handed me the key. He then headed back down the staircase to greet another customer. I grinned at the thought of our perfect seclusion. The floor creaked with each step as we approached the suite. The sound escalated my excitement, as I knew the secret of her destiny. When I opened the door, the vaulted ceilings, draped with elegantly hung tapestries, along with the perfectly positioned candles, awed me and heightened the mood. *If I could love someone,* I mused, *I would build them a chamber like this. Love? Did I reference love?* Pushing aside my irrelevant thoughts, I locked the door.

At last, we were alone, with no one to ruin this magnificent occasion. I drew a whisper from my mouth that only a dark soul could hear. "How shall we begin?" I solicited. She gave me a perplexed look. Abruptly her inner demon took over as the appetite in her eyes swelled and voracity filled her desolate soul. In the corner of the room stood a bed with a canopy. I seized her icy hand and led her on a journey, which she energetically supported. All the while, a wave of rapidity swept over me. The bed was well suited for the occasion; attached to the posts were long decorative ribbons, which proved quite handy in securing her hands and feet to the bed's poster frame. As she struggled, I drew my handkerchief from my pocket and shoved it in her swinelike mouth to muffle her pleas. You may wonder about her devilish eyes. To ease your curiosity, I will let you know I left her eyes uncovered so she too could witness my evolution toward glory. The thought of watching her draw her last breath aroused me. Without a moment to squander, I unfastened her corset. Why not do the deed with her clothing intact? Because the desires of society had polluted her attire, it demanded banishment. To her, the clothes' purpose was not to protect others from catching her nudity but to show a status of gross affluence.

With every inch of clothing torn from her body, my adrenaline escalated, facilitating my power. I had little interest in learning the cattle's name, for they possess no redeeming qualities that have earned them the privilege. I caressed her hair to suggest an illusion of human compassion. My fingers started from her scalp and traveled down her exposed back, tracing every fleshy nook; I wished to etch her figure's roadmap in my mind. As I stroked her crimson locks with my wasp-like fingertips, I peered into her scarlet eyes, noting that, like her hair, they mimicked the fiery pits of hell. Repulsed, I jumped back. She did not deserve even the slightest trace of human care, for I had deemed her a beast and a blight on humanity. From my peripheral vision, I noticed the corner of the room grow dark with misery. It was Father. He had arrived, his presence reminding me of our purpose. Only he should ever possess my devotion. She was cacodemon, bearing a ludicrous mask of human likeness. I shifted my eyes back from Father to the target fixed on the bed, and as God as my witness, I saw her eyes transform, revealing her inner monster. Little did she know I alone owned the hands to decide her consequence. I needed to move quickly before her master made his hourly prowl.

As my eyes swept across the suite, it appeared the room was turning in circles as I desperately searched for weapons. Why did I not consider these details in advance? Infuriated panic gathered in front of me like an unsuspecting ship heading toward an iceberg. My head was ablaze as the beating echo of my pulse grew deafening. I became anxious over the possibility that the thunderous pounding would arouse others from their slumber, allowing them to bear witness to the horror. Suddenly I heard a foreign sound, mirroring that of a sizable marble moving across the floor. From the most profound depth of the dark shadow-filled corner emerged a rolling bottle of wine. What was I to do with a bottle of wine? I did not want to make a mess but had little time to waste. Thinking quickly, I seized the bottle and struck its neck against one of the bedposts, crudely shearing the top. I then snatched a handful of her hair and forcefully tilted her head back at a sharp angle, snapping her neck. Uncertain whether her twitching was a sign of life or death, I finished the deed by removing my handkerchief from her mouth and pouring the smooth red liquid down her nose and throat. The room's glow gave one last flash of light across her eyes, and with a final gasping breath, the cow drowned in her own self-pity. Her wicked, lifeless gawp inspired me to spit in her face. I unbound her limbs and placed the prized handkerchief in my pocket. Then I tucked her in and propped her eyes open to provide Father the perfect setting for devouring her soulless desires.

My first kill! This occasion marked my life's beginning. Do not fret; you may think I am cruel, but I gave the animal what she desired. As I left, I tossed a few schillings onto the bed. All whores deserve payment for their services. Darkness filled the air with a sense of purpose as I turned into a behemoth of a man. Churchgoers believe the power of a man's soul diminishes with murder, but this is far from the truth.

You may ask what might spur a man to face demonization. The simple answer is hypocrites! Those who demonize others and continue to lie about loving humanity are the hypocrites of our society. They harp on every little meddling point regarding ideas to save their fellow man but lack the inspiration to act. They are devoid of compassion, and their blight blocks their ability to experience someone who ensnares and cradles their souls at night. I have reaped the rewards of my willingness to act. I am blessed with someone who fights for me and takes what is theirs right out from under their very chin. The same chin that allows their filthy mouths to open wide and spew hate. The pathetic among us are ignored, especially by those who take more than they can swallow at supper and spit at those who beg. They will atone for their apathy. I am not perfect, but I am above the animals of class. I will be their great savior or the greatest fear that haunts them every night until they succumb to their deliverance. I am the dark owl born of no soul.

With confidence, I removed my handkerchief from my pocket to smell the victory. As the stench hit my nose, I couldn't help but look into the eyes of the dark cobblestone way that lay lifeless under my feet. *I am home*, I thought. *I am Daniel Manly.*

Two

WHAT A SHITHOLE

Carriages clattered in the darkness as their loose hinges moaned like the whores that inhabited the pitiless cobblestone streets. The night grew black as dusk set, the lamplight highlighting my chiseled jawline. Frigid air caressed my muscled neck, causing its tendons to tighten like vicious boa constrictors. The sensation made my jaw clench with pleasure. Contentment ran through every vessel of my body and boiled from my nostrils. As the tautening continued, I grew smitten and grinned, my smile emulating that of a giddy child. Carnal tension in my throat made my blood blister. The erotic rush gave me that sensation that life was being removed from my body with each searing breath.

The clattering sounds escalated as additional coaches joined the screeching parade of carriage wheels abrading the cobblestones. the cruel fate of the passengers made me quiver, not from fear but excitement at the exhibition I was about to witness. I chuckled at the thought of icy bodies dropping to their stone-laden graves. Again the rattling slapped the side of my ears, causing my thoughts to silence. The sounds of the horses' footsteps masked my plan, expanded my confidence, and replaced every inch of diffidence. The music continued to orchestrate the lifeless streets with hooves playing melodic patterns that soothed me. Like a newborn pup sucking on its mother's tit, I felt the warmth of security. The ornate quilt thrown upon my shoulders was from the very streets I once degraded with cursing words.

Brick walls made up the buildings that guided the cobblestone path as the feeble light brought focus to the scenic route. The annoying luminosity sprouted from large crippling lampposts leading unknowing wanderers astray down a counterfeit path of safety. I gazed into the blaze; my squinting eyes blinded with foreboding. Unkind, the lights served as unwelcoming warning signals, unveiling every torturous secret of the night. Proceeding through the cobblestone maze, I couldn't help continuing to look up at the light illuminating my way. Was it the light of goodness or a charlatan of darkness? The flame triggered thoughts of reemergence through firelight, filling my soul with adrenaline. My body quaked with anticipation.

Darkness had devoured my soul's light long ago in the same way a bony man gobbles a hearty goulash filled with fresh meat. Like a battered piece of driftwood embraced by the sea, I was enveloped and swathed by shadows. I felt content with the companionship from the shadows but continued to notice the light's captivation with my presence. It appeared as if the two contrasting friends were fighting for my soul. The luminosity's fascination struck me as flattering. An identical illumination had flashed through the eyes of the redheaded wench with her last moo. She too had witnessed the battle between light and dark. For a moment the heifer's gaze had held a fighting spark veiled by the darkness like cold, murky water drowning a weak flame. The last labored gasp of her devilish breath had painted a beautiful portrait of new beginnings.

With a snap of my fingers and clap of my hands, I beckoned a carriage. As my exquisite hand passed the brim of my hat, my glove tightened. The stark white glove against my creamy pale skin would entice any carriage gent to stop his steeds. A screeching halt pierced the musky air, slicing the fog like a serrated knife cutting freshly baked bread.

The glistening stallions conveyed their disdain with intolerable grunts of disapproval. Engrossed by the light that now peered around my waiting ride, I edged my way to the carriage, my boots echoing louder than the horses' hooves pawing at the ground. A thundering heartbeat eclipsed all other sounds. Was I imagining things? Was it possible this reverberation was coming from the core of my being? Hunting prey was exhilarating--the very prey that encompasses all that is wicked in this vile world. Thank God I was here to put such creatures out of their misery. "Let us consummate this grand occasion with a toast," I murmured to myself, chuckling. I was one with the surrounding darkness.

I bellowed to the elderly driver, demanding that he remain patient. As I did, I noted the tone of my summoning had chilled his bones to ice. Assuring his compliance, I realigned my line of sight to the steps leading into the shadowy carriage. The slightly ajar door revealed the cabin's darkness and a glimpse into my grimly soothing destiny, which comforted me.

As I stepped into the carriage and adjusted my position, a familiar warmth oozed to my left; the dark shadow I found so dear was beside me. As murky blackness overtook the outer shell of my corneas, a vast and menacing grin came across my face, my lips parting so slowly that even mortar drying would win the race. With a crack of the driver's whip, our journey began. The stallions pulled violently at their bridles as if trying to escape the evening's looming events. The wind intensified, causing the carriage to viciously sway, each convulsion propelling me forward on my mission. My bony fingers parted the curtains at the window beside me. As I peered through the leaded glass, I made out a hand-painted sign in the distance. The disgraceful sign appeared as though someone had vomited talentless passion upon an undesirable piece of wood. Unappealing flowers adorned the abomination to convince dubious visitors that the town offered dainty, fair-skinned maidens who enjoyed nothing more than strolling through a garden. The bird shit covering the welcome should have provided evidence enough that the "perfect" town was a sham. Squinting, I barely made out the name that lay amid the crackling paint. "Welcome to Northburry," I sang to myself. I chuckled as I contemplated whether the dilapidated sign knew what it had been helping to conceal. In mere hours the morning light would reveal every misjudgment of the night and warn everyone of the dangers associated with my undying attention.

Passing the atrocious artwork, I continued to size up the scenery that entered my minuscule portal to the outside world. The small dusty window was my opportunity to imprint the structure of my new home within my skull matter. With cunning wit, I ran multiple scenarios through my mind and adjusted myself in my seat. My mood rested on a razor's edge as I determined when it would be most advantageous to pounce on my prey and relinquish my soul to the creeping darkness. The horses drew to a merciless stop within the town's gates, their hooves hitting the cobblestones, creating a superficial sound announcing that Northburry befittingly lay on shallow ground. Glowing fire from a nearby lantern illuminated the path, revealing the secrets of the night's shadows. The light's purity shone vibrantly as if trying to push away the darkness from its leaded-glass windows. I liken the light to my soul purging the trash-filled streets of all polluting entities.

My thick skull ached in disbelief over my calling's importance. Like magic, the driver appeared and opened the door to let me know he had stopped to take a piss. The light of the nearby streetlamp filled the cabin, tormenting the darkness--my only friend, my father, the only love I would ever know. I vowed to extinguish my tormentor, squeeze until air could no longer assist the defiant candle's dimming wick. As it struggled to regain life and continue to burn, I would not relent. I galloped off my seat and glanced at the cobblestones the horses anxiously heaved upon. The stained trail appeared dingy and unsympathetic, with weather-beaten cracks. Did you know you can tell a town's story by its cobblestones? Every action and secret of the characters are recorded as they grace the cold stone paths.

It was time to begin. I closed my eyes for a moment and swore I heard a deep exhalation behind me, signaling that Father was delighted the purge was about to ensue. "The piggish, self-indulgent shall fall, and their ungrateful souls shall not be missed," the darkness whispered. I knew Father was right. After relieving himself, the driver apathetically moved back to the carriage, checking my only piece of luggage. I do not travel heavy and am quite precise in assuring I perfectly plan the items I pack for each day's happenings. The driver's filthy, piss-covered hands fingered the carved ivory handle of my bag as he tussled with my luggage, making sure it was secure. When I observed him more closely, I realized he had a noticeably strange limp that, when analyzed, was most likely caused by an event related to his sordid past. A thick beard lay on his face, crumb laden and unkempt.

"Begin," I heard a raspy whisper behind me. As the driver continued to touch my bag with his filthy, mangled, piglike fingers, I was desperate for him to liberate it, but my outrage prevented me from releasing the command from my mouth. Searching my walking stick for answers, I embraced it like a baton of gold. My cane, my trusted companion for many years, would provide the words my mouth was not ready to utter.

With great swiftness, I exited the carriage, elevated the walking stick above my head, and swung down with the force of a giant. The impact to the man's skull was so extraordinary that it knocked him to his knees and caused me a terrible pain that trailed from my clenched jaw to my pale knuckles. Appalled at the thought that his tainted fluid would leak out, creating a bloody river of truth, I made sure my ensuing blows fell squarely on his back, intending to limit his pleas for help by beating the wind out of him. The minute or five of the swift, strategic blows of my ingenious method of attack eased any risk that his lungs would release enough air to generate so much as a peep. You may wonder why I noted such a time discrepancy when showcasing the beating. In the occurrence's moment, I became lost in the depths of my mind, and the wickedness of pain and sorrow overtook my actions. The closest emulation of the feeling would come from being in a catatonic state with crows pecking the inner edges of my eyes without my even noticing.

Crows are mysterious creatures that harbor great darkness in their shiny black coats and mock the world with predatory sounds from meager beaks.

With every flap, enchanted wings take a familiar route toward their prey, gliding through the air with purpose. Their narrowing path leaves no question regarding their intent for their spotted target. Fear accumulates as the inevitable becomes a reality, causing the intended victim to cuff the air like a maiden latching her bedchamber door to protect her chaste treasures from a ravenous man. I resemble the referenced crow--the only difference being that I have a weightier existence and less pluckiness. Though crows only live a mere fifteen years, they are formidable hunters, and nothing remains safe from their vivacious feeding holes. I do not oppose their feasting on fresh blood and skin that writhe with the nightmares of gruesome pecks. You may wonder why I am so infatuated with these wondrous creatures. Many believe the sight of a single crow can foretell death and misfortune; I spit on the souls of the obtuse who tell such imbecilic lies. Pragmatic notions spew an abundance of absurdities in life. It is grievous that an object's color defines its value and treatment in society. Regardless of society's opinions, the shadow and the crow bring me a vast amount of comfort. Both of their dark exteriors coincide with my psyche. To me, sighting a beautiful black crow fortifies my optimistic ideas.

A longing gasp of the musky air replaced my pleasant thoughts of crows with the reality that had previously consumed my attention. The coachman's breathing took on the sound of a burning village as his malformed gaze fixed on my scarcely disheveled appearance. For a moment his voice expressed all the glorious qualities I imagined one's soul might make if one were drowning for air. Although the beating was enthralling, the residual gasping infuriated me; why would he not be quiet? With each draw of putrid air he took, my scorching blood rose to my weighty skull. Did he not care others were trying to sleep? His selfish noise oozed narcissism, his self–centered actions and embarrassing animation consuming my angry thoughts. How dare he think he stood taller than the night's comforting blanket of solitude! Furiously I paced near the old man. My patience on a razor's edge, I stopped for a moment, staring into his devilish eyes, as if I might see him differently. The pupils that caught my study offered a direct view of his pitiful soul. This carriage master was nothing more than a pile of demon excrement.

Without a second thought, I raised the cane once more in utter annoyance, taking my place as the conductor of hell's symphonic orchestra. The man's infuriating gasps became an imposition to the harmonious finale and disturbed an otherwise lovely evening. I would not allow myself to let him ruin the coherent harmony! Cuing the cymbals at the back of the room, I swung harder than I had in all previous blows combined. I enjoyed watching as my gold stick made an excellent crackling sound as it struck against his jugular. My ears' disappointment quickly extinguished my excitement, though, as the sound bore a striking resemblance to that of a tambourine rather than the dynamic cymbal I had expected.

Aware of the magnitude of my actions, however, I noted a sense of contentment reenter my thoughts.

I couldn't help feeling impressed by my many hidden talents! Sneering, I pictured myself, a budding musician, debuting his newfound skill across the ribs of a degenerate carcass. Did anyone else witness my bare hands orchestrating the most magnificent concerto, complementing an already perfect night sky? I wished not to be the only one to know of my outstanding talent. Who knew I was so well-rounded? Maybe an added whack would allow me to seize the favor of any potential audience that faltered in the chilly night.

At last, the old man's maddening sounds no longer disrupted the murky air. Many would assume I struck him again for assurance, but it was purely for amusement, to be quite honest. Granting him three long seconds, I realized he, in fact, was lifeless. With the ease of gathering trash from a kitchen floor, I lifted the filthy limp remains and carried them back to the carriage.

The body was light as a feather and stiff as a board. The insignificant gravity made it seem like a throng of invisible pallbearers had joined hands to help deliver this cockroach to his last resting place. In an instant, my eyes targeted the wagon's backside storage compartment. The compartment's hinges groaned with delight as I lifted the lid and tossed the carcass into the black cavity. The embellished casing shut with the sound of applause when the lame body caressed the black-velvet interior. I clapped my hands three times to join in on the fun and cheerfully made my way to the front of the carriage. There was one last thing I had to do. Before me stood a grotesque yet familiar observer, a glowing lantern atop an ornate iron post. My analysis felt different from before; now, instead of intrigue, I felt irrepressible rage. Narrowing my focus, I took a jagged detour and headed toward the taunting flame that mocked my existence. With a gust of air leaving my lips, I put an end to its miserable life. "Ha!" Chuckles of delight rang through my soul. The light never stood a chance against my cold wrath. At last, there was no more brightness to grace the town's desires; it had been extinguished for good. If only the residents knew that the light I had snuffed out on this eve was the world's only truthful overseer. The town was my kingdom, bending to my every whim.

With my agitated thoughts cradled, an invigorated pep fueled my every stride. I felt at ease as I marched back to the carriage, ready to take my rightful throne. Noticing my coattails had become a bit tousled, I smoothed out the fabric before stepping into the carriage. Then, with great confidence and a solidified sense of purpose, I hopped into the driver's seat, opened my throat wide, and let out a significant hiss to signal the horses. Thanks to Father, I now had a beautiful barouche. *How grand*, I thought. "It is quite ironic. The man who has always had to walk now has the best seat in the house," I said, chuckling. Twinkling at the notion that the darkness knew how to quench my thirst and provide for my every need, I brandished a tooth-filled grin as I wondered, *How could I possibly be a desirable man without a grand carriage?* I assessed the expensive ride I had secured and marveled at the excellent steeds that pulled me toward the night's calling.

The shadow's warmth encompassed me. I was in my rightful transportation, pulled by magnificent creatures. I let out a calming breath that smelled of contentment and reveled in the sanctuary Father had provided. A town emerged past the view of the horses' groomed ears. "Northburry, I am home," I whispered to the night sky as it dashed past the carriage.

"You are home," a deep voice chimed in return. The melodic tune had arisen from the coaches dark passenger compartment. The voice's validation solidified the knowledge that I had no choice in the matter; a providence greater than my own had predestined it. Northburry was beckoning me like a siren.

Although I had no written directions for my destination, I knew Father would guide me. The brief glimpses of my future through recurrent dreams had built great anticipation. Piercing my nightly visions, the estate had become the only image that marched through my head each evening. Brick walls, blood-red as a butcher's table, were bound by mustard-colored mortar. Masculine shrubs lined the complacent drive that led to the grandly carved dark entryway. The dungeon-like doors would entice any sleepwalker to wander in during a catatonic stroll. The windows above the colosseum-size pillars played whistling interludes as the wind caught their edges. Large brushing vines adorned with small pearl-like flowers surrounded the house's picturesque borders. From the vivid imagery, I knew the path to be followed. Merged as one with the shadowy night, the two steeds chewed at their bits, sensing every ounce of danger.

The demon-fueled horses pulled my sitting corpse and restless feet forward as they picked up haste toward our destination. The shadows made the path so unmistakable that hell's carriage could drive there alone. At last, I sighted an illuminated path off the primary drive, just as it had appeared in my dreams. The warming light functioned as a beacon for fluttering moths to signal the way to the magnificent property. The sizable estate provided enough enticement to lure women into giving up every ounce of their morality for an opportunity to be the "lady" of the house. No one would decline my proposal of marriage in this godforsaken town; I was an irresistible package that any woman of sound mind would not refuse. The extravagant six-bedchamber and six-powder-room estate would fool any onlooker regarding my wealth and mask the reality that perdition lay just beyond the doorway.

Adorned with large crystal chandeliers and carved ceilings, the ballroom and formal dining room were nothing short of spectacular. To the left side of the entry stood the study. From my dreams, I knew this would become my favorite place for reflection. The previous owner had spent only one summer at the estate countless years before my arrival and had passed away in a distant township. As he had no heirs and hadn't built connections with the residents of Northburry, his timely disappearance had gone unnoticed. All his belongings remained in place, right down to the imported place settings and fine linens. Alas, for the first time in my atrocious life, someone had tended to my every need.

Tonight I would sleep; tomorrow I would emerge reborn.

Three

THE CHATTERS

Night lifted from the colorless scene. Wide awake, I didn't remember walking through the grand gates of the estate, but my eyes opened to find an ornate bedroom greeting me. "Oh, happy day," I exclaimed as I stretched my palms into the sky and gave each fist a squeeze. My glee was of true intent, my voice colored with more precise diction than usual. As dawn appeared, an unstoppable light gleamed through the skyline of brick walls that held the town together. The spectral eye of the light forced its way into my chamber, spying on my sedentary frame through the bedroom window. As the light hit my flesh, I knew the bodies of others were warming as well on the other side of the small town. I couldn't help being engulfed by my curious nature, and trust me when I say, "Curiosity does not kill the cat."

The sky held no clouds, allowing the bright light from the early sunrise to reveal not only the contents of my bedroom but also four unremarkable women gathering for tea within the sunroom of a grand stone cottage estate that dripped with dancing vines.

As they banded together like a pack of ravenous vultures, I visualized them sitting in any meager room, devouring all reputations that traversed their path. While they performed frivolous activities they deemed as high societal talents, their noxious feasts ruined lives in a matter of moments.

They were chattering, soulless creatures who cared for no one and found great amusement in discussing others' misfortunes. Who were they to gossip about the town's other residents? Were their own lives not lively enough? Were they content with their self-absorbed lives or was their off-putting behavior a toxic mask to cover up their irrefutable misery? I believe they rejoiced in the opportunity to play cruel games, seeing who could squish the innocent spider first. The irony is that the same spider might be the catalyst for their demise. Protecting their inheritance and accompanying social status at all costs was their principal goal, for without a grand estate, there was no identity. The light captured and exposed their souls, revealing a despicable shallowness like that of a succubus and nothing more.

The women in the Bonnet family were not decent, nor were they what young babes should strive to become. No example of inner beauty was ever-present in their proceeding lineage; as a result, I considered every family member rotten. They were cowards in denial of their own inadequacies, filling the troughs of their shortcomings with insincerity and revelry over the bad luck of others. These women were monsters. *Monsters*! I connect their vileness to bugs that, when squished, ooze their juices onto the bottom of my handmade leather shoes. Their overconfidence was intoxicating to the weak-minded creatures of the world, allowing them to shepherd any sheep-infested pasture. In listening company, these propagators of hateful renditions of etiquette vomited enticing words from their gaping mouths, sending desperate suitors into trancelike states and causing them to respond with unconscious nods of agreement.

I relate the toxic stupor created by these women to the effects one may experience by taking up residence in a field of poppies. Words can make grown men high and young boys weak. The opioid effect of maidens masks their poisonous verbiage for most pathetic men seeking betrothal. I, however, see the truth, and their words in no way resemble harmonious singing. Instead, every word they utter pollutes the air with tortuous shrieks that are comparable to that of a dove being strangled by the most grotesque of serpents. The same viper that damned Adam and Eve to misery.

Who were these women to judge every person they encountered by their financial assets alone? The family would gasp if a bishop said, "Monetary wealth is of underwhelming importance when considering character." Even a bishop of their own corrupted church could not sway them otherwise. They were paltry little sea urchins, so small they should have hidden in fear of how shallow the water would become. Once the quenching liquids tide receded, they would shrivel like prunes on a hot summer day. Before I bore you with my exhilarating banter, let me introduce you, one by one, to the revolting cattle that lived at their ever-so-grand Northbury estate. Five bodies took up space in the home--six if you included the indentured servant. The residents included a father, mother, three eligible daughters, and a servant who was of little significance because of her minimalistic life and inability to marry due to her indentured status. Anything could change, but for now she was no threat to the core of the world, so I shall leave her alone. I shall place my focus on the family that dwelt at the estate. I felt like I had hit the jackpot since all three daughters were on a desperate hunt to harpoon a beneficial suitor. Of the three daughters, one was considered the most prized possession. If the parents had lined up their daughters in a trophy case, she would have sat on the top shelf because her attributes aligned with what society considered the highest marital value.

Grace was the youngest of the three frenetic cows, considered God's golden trophy by her parents. Bouncing blond ringlets effortlessly heightened the fifteen-year-old's beautiful complexion as she restitched bland needlework. The swine that raised her and forced her to wean too early from the sow's shriveled tit touted her beauty across the town as if she were the prize heifer at a county fair. The piggy parents considered her the prettiest in the countryside and made sure they vocalized this notion. They wanted the immediate family and every bystander who would lend an ear to believe her reputation for beauty would garner the most shillings on the marital auction block. Believing God had given Grace to the family as a "humbling gift," the mother had thought her beauty a miracle because she considered her other daughters to have misfortunate appearances. Her being born to the earth confirmed to the parents that their acts of hypocritical piety successfully achieved God's favor. Grace's birth was the reason behind her parents' expanded love for the church and increased spectacle of avid attendance.

The weekly mass served as a selfish confessional for the largest sow of them all, the mother. She wanted to assure that her greatest wishes were both known and granted in a typical narcissistic fashion. Every week she spewed prayers to the heavens, not for the betterment of humankind but to feign purity and ensure the fruition of her extensive list of desires. Her facade of reverence was only intended to mask her devilish life. Believe my words when I tell you her true personality lay hidden from the public eye. The light stood witness to her lack of sympathy when casting away the homeless, uncaring as they lay on the ground writhing with hunger. When witnessing her genuine behavior, no man in his right mind would consider any of her heinous traits those of a godly woman. If Grace hadn't been the fruit of her womb, the name "God" or any other associated devotion would not dare continue to touch her lips or those of any family member who lived under the household's roof. Grace was the most likely to marry well and bring riches upon the undeserving, despicable family. As a well-bred woman, the cattle's primary goal is to snare a man of elevated societal status, and she would do that with ease. With Grace's picturesque physique and high-set rose-colored cheeks, marrying more advantageously than her two elder sisters would prove effortless.

The loathsome woman's point of view regarding her daughters can be compared to a trophy case. On the second shelf sits sixteen-year-old Eve, the middle daughter, whom her mother considered a secondhand piece of metal semi-resembling a trophy. As she sat painting a portrait of fruit due to her lack of talent in needlework, she looked at her younger sister with sinful jealousy. Eve was short in stature, appeared sweet with meek features and dirty blond waves that refused to keep perfect curls to accent her slightly off-color porcelain skin. Eve held the firm position as the unyielding middle fixture of this dysfunctional family. If a suitor were unsuccessful in soliciting the youngest daughter's affection, she would be the backup plan in terms of selections. No one in Northburry wanted her as an in-law to their family's crest, but none felt the need to complain at her mildly beautiful stature. Though she was nowhere near Grace in terms of looks, both parents chose this daughter to be considered their firstborn because of her better-than-average chance of securing a viable spouse. The child did not resemble the perfect porcelain dolls her mother had positioned in the nursery's ornate wooden curio cabinet. When setting her hopeful eyes for the first time on her newborn's face, she knew the child would not meet her standard of beauty.

When a mother lays eyes on their newborn, they fall in love, but instead of loving thoughts, a name befitting a mediocre child came to mind: Eve. Since the child was delivered during nightfall and the morning was the sow's most precious time of day, she preferred not to associate a name that signified a comparison to her favorite hour with a child whose facial structure was not a divine sight. Upon the baby's birth she had a revelation: she believed the name Eve was the most thoughtful compromise she could muster. As an afterthought, she touted that she had chosen the name out of reverence to God and believed God would show her divine favor for her selection. Eve's parents, however, forgot about her after her toddler years because Grace arrived.

I have skimmed over the two most relevant trophies, according to the parents; only one remains, Hope. She was the third and eldest beast and, turning the age of eighteen, by far the least-prized trophy. As Hope hid in a corner of the room, her birdlike features, tiny black eyes, and black falling updo peeked out above a short novel that engulfed her. Although she was born first, the Bonnets did not consider her as such. Hope was the narcissistic sow's greatest disappointment, and in the trophy case scenario, she would hold a place on the floor beneath the cabinet. You may find the parents' description of their own flesh and blood disconcerting. Some may wonder why any parent would cast aside their eldest child and claim their middle child as the first of the family line. That is because the creature born as the medically recorded eldest daughter was peculiar. You could say she walked alone on an unconventional path, and to make matters worse, she bore little to no resemblance to either parent. Her parents did not name her based on status or beauty but ambition, which was considered an unattractive attribute for a woman.

Believe me when I say she was the greatest embarrassment the heavens had dropped on the swine couples' righteous laps. The mother's initial gaze into her eldest child's eyes caused her to cry out, not in sadness but out of selfish repudiation. When the baby was born, panic reverberated through her body as she summoned a priest. She felt the babe had been handed to her by mistake or Satan himself had placed this hideous child in her life as a cruel joke. Had she not been praying enough to bypass this fateful lesson? The mother saw all her wrongdoings flash like lightning before her eyes. She wished to repent for anything that had caused this scar on her vanity. During her pleading to God and through her newfound holiness, she settled on naming the child "Hope." Hope symbolized their banishment of negativity; it also signified the rebirth of religious rituals for the family, along with their desire to improve the outcome of any subsequent births. By fashioning a godlier outward appearance, they believed their successive children would be the blessings they deserved. From that point forward, they spun all negative thoughts of Hope's presence into benedictions, preaching to the town only of her kindness. They were convinced positive affirmations would someday relieve their parental obligations by securing her a man and a new permanent home. In their wicked minds, they thought the words falling from their tongues rang as charity.

Now that we have completed our introduction of the daughters, let's move on to the woman who birthed them. The matriarch I refer to as the "sow" was the vilest in the herd. Her grotesque carcass thrived in the murky pits of society and dwelt wherever greed and hatred found solace. The overdressed sow flourished by devouring the best of human attributes and polluting the earth with her malevolent dung. They gave the sow a birth name I refuse to disclose because of its potential for evoking compassion for the demon. Even whispering the word into the air might risk humanization by weak souls. Do not sympathize with the cow!

I must admit having a reference for her other than "cow," "sow," etc. will improve the convenience of my storytelling, so I will reveal a name that bears no tie to her birth, a name she gained through the legal arrangement with her husband. Her married name now and forever is Mrs. Bonnet. If asked who she most resembled, the cow would emphatically state, her trophy spawn, but her resemblance truly was somewhere between that of Hope and Eve. The insufferable animal had dull blond hair with frizzed ends that she attempted to tame with dirty rosewater, while her other physical attributes were those of a lame horse. That is all the information I will provide, for she is undeserving of anything more. Through this tale, you will not shed a tear for the undeserving matriarch. She married for greed and, with her decision, gave up the right of happiness and compassion. Mrs. Bonnet was apathetic to her daughters' happiness, encouraging them to follow in her footsteps and become the miserable pets of wealthy men. Her resentment toward them stemmed greatly from the fact that she believed God had cheated her by not giving her a male heir. Since a father's inheritance can only pass from male to male, birthing a son was necessary in assuring she would reap the benefits of wealth and societal position if she were widowed. Though she wished for her husband's premature departure every minute of every day, she knew the reality of that wish would fuck her. Not having a son trapped her in a much-deserved purgatory. For that reason, among others, she loathed her firstborn since she started the chain of bad luck.

In my explicit opinion, which I know you all fancy, this story has become too estrogen filled for my liking. Where is the male figure, and why has the man not made a grand appearance? He was not without culpability as he fueled his wife's insatiable desires, yielding to her every whim and evading her childish tantrums. Mr. Bonnet, the father of the house, was a coward who ate his meals alone and maintained at least a room's distance from the monsters he had created. Seeing their faces every day became too painful for him to bear, their manipulative whines scratching his ears like sharpened daggers. When night fell and the clock struck the honeymoon hour, you would find him sleeping alone in his study.

Mr. Bonnet's face exhibited a leathered appearance from his weathering the cow's narcissistic demands over the years. Alcohol was his chosen method of masking his self-pity over the shit life he had created. The women who surrounded him knew neither what he was like without alcohol on his breath or a staggering step. For this reason, he rarely attended social functions. His day started at sunrise, sequestered behind the locked door of his office, obscured from the judging eyes that bulged at his uncontrollable guzzling of whatever vile liquid he could grasp with his groveling fingers. Numbness entered his body with every swallow. Each swig allowed him to emulate feelings of peace to his core. Each day, the euphoric detachment temporarily jailed his wild running thoughts and gave him false hope for an altered tomorrow.

Enough time wasted on a man responsible for creating such a sizable flock of abysmal creatures! The Bonnet women routinely strolled through the besmirched town, spending pennies on vanity and putting their haughtiness on display at all forms of gatherings. Determined to find proper suitors, the herd maintained a steady prowl through public venues, searching for signs of wealth and societal elevation. Like a lioness stalking its prey to slaughter, Mrs. Bonnet led her cubs in a daily hunt for beneficial matches, a quest that proved to be their only ambition in their irrelevant lives.

My thoughts returned to the illustrious cobblestone street that had become a cherished marker for my valiant calling. I paused for a moment, reveling at the streetlamp that remained unlit, its darkness continuing to shroud me from prying eyes. I imagined Northburry's residents taking part in toxic idle chatter as they passed the Gothic lamppost, unaware of its murderous secret. The Bonnet sisters had made a grand appearance, noses in the air and fashionably late to the livestock parade, their bustles swaying side to side in their hopes of luring wealthy wandering eyes. Their intentional movements left no question about this, as they were deft in the efficacious use of their feminine wiles. My mental observation of the morose scene lasted for seven clicks of the minute hand on my pocket watch, giving me ample time to make an accurate judgment.

Well rested and full of vigor, I leaped from my luxurious mahogany bed and pushed back the golden velvet curtains that elegantly hung over the street-side window. Carriages clattered, and townspeople cackled with laughter as they passed my impressive estate; it was surprising to find such a level of activity in the early-morning hours. I was not remiss in saying "my impressive estate"; as I have said before, Father provides for my every need. The estate's new life created quite a stir among the town's residents, with the Bonnet herd speculating about the mysterious resident's identity. If a guessing game is what they wanted, a guessing game was what they would get. Father had provided details regarding their social tendencies, and they were quite predictable. I knew when they would perform their sickening hunt for riches.

Already prepped by Father's intuition, I had been anticipating the spectacle that was soon to come. The light now trickled more harshly on my face as I stood by the window looking down at my pocket watch, waiting for the hands to reach 10:00 a.m. It was time! They did not disappoint. At 10:00 a.m. on the mark, I closed my eyes to shield myself from the light and glimpse into the town's flesh-consumed thoughts. Like clockwork the Bonnet daughters' routine began as they paraded by like qualified prostitutes in bustling skirts, stopping for a moment to glance at my estate, hoping to glimpse the mystery proprietor. Trying to look higher-class, Mrs. Bonnet had attempted to dress up each of their muted pastel dresses with vibrant peacock-feather hairpieces. The only visual aspect that might have made their intentions more blatantly clear would have been for each of the whores to drop and spread their legs for suitors to get a better look at their offerings.

Mrs. Bonnet stood nearby, looking smug as she filled the role of the ringleader of the comedic featured act that starred three clowns portraying whores in search of husbands. If the opportunity presented itself, the cow herself would off her husband and remarry for higher status. She oozed a sense of self-importance, the rancidity smelling of an unjustified God complex. "Come along," she shrieked. Strutting farther up the cobblestone street, Mrs. Bonnet noticed Hope had smuggled a book, and while trying to read its contents, she had trailed behind. Raising her hand, the woman signaled for the girls to stop and briskly walked to the back of the line. Realizing Hope still hadn't paid attention, Mrs. Bonnet pinched her arm. "Tardiness is never a good attribute, girl," she hissed. "Learn from your mistakes." Mrs. Bonnet scowled as Hope cringed in pain. Desperate to reclaim her position as the head of the cattle line, the girls' mother swatted Grace's hunched spine to straighten it. Continuing with their stroll, they made their way to a storefront. Trifling with potential suitors wasn't the only reason they were in town that day. Mrs. Bonnet determined that the girls' lack of expensive accouterments was why they had remained husbandless. She clearly was quite obsessed with the mysterious bachelor and was hell-bent on assuring that one of her daughters won the prize. What better way to lure a match than to don lavish accessories that leave not an ounce of mystery regarding your lofty societal position?

I laughed at the absurdity as I watched the circus from my window. Little did the Bonnets know the "new guest" they had been gossiping about had been observing the lot for the better part of two days. If they only knew of my abominable upbringing and the irony that I had been deemed the most eligible bachelor in this mediocre town! I skipped around my isolated room with joy, my gambols jolly and menacing; I did not require music to inspire my dance. Even without meeting me in person, they already were swooning over my affluence. Absent of Father's presence, I would still be a cockroach crawling about on the urine-filled streets. Now, however, I was the most unstoppable force to grace the earth's soil and the only one to reap the rewards of Father's love and attention. The vilest of the town would soon understand that money is not a virtue.

Reaching the tailor shop, all four of the women admired the ornate dresses in the window. Stepping on Eve's toe, Grace attempted to get the first look at the garments to stake claim on what she felt was rightfully hers. Annoyed by the lack of service, Mrs. Bonnet aggressively knocked on the fogged shop window. A yawning older man in a fitted suit unlocked the storefront and invited them inside. Pushing past him, Mrs. Bonnet immediately made her way to the new fabric swatches. "Are you trying to give us a conniption?" she dramatically shrilled. Turning up their noses, Grace and Eve copied their mother's behavior while Hope avoided eye contact with the man. As they rummaged through the store, the owner was overjoyed at how much they were grotesquely spending. With a tap on Eve's shoulder, Grace pointed to the window that housed the dresses on display and laughed at the miscellaneous clothing styles. Feeling as though she were missing out on a jolly time, Mrs. Bonnet eagerly joined in with the girls, snatching a girdle and passing it to Eve. "We all know who'll need this," she said with a gleam in her eye. Grace smirked while making piglike noises to mock Eve.

Irritated, Eve grabbed the girdle and, using the momentum, smacked Grace's bosom. "Oh dear," Eve said with a shrug.

Miffed at her sister's retaliation, Grace reacted with a glare. "You presumptuous cow. You did that on purpose!" her lips exuded loud enough for her mother to hear as she shoved Eve into the display hats.

You might wonder where the mother was in all this mess. Rather than nip the tussle in the bud, Mrs. Bonnet looked smug as she proudly filled the role of orchestrator. She smirked with her hands raised. "Girls, we must focus on what is important," she said while caressing a roll of silk hanging on the wall. Regaining their attention, she pointed to numerous fabrics she wished to buy. Satisfied with her selections, she adjusted her multilayered petticoat and marched toward the exit. Angered that no one had followed her to the door, she quickly grew annoyed. "Come along, girls!" she yelled in a fit of temper. Worried they would lose their mother's monetary favor, Grace and Eve pushed over each other as they rushed to the door. After clearing her throat, Mrs. Bonnet turned toward a stagnant Hope. "That includes you," she snapped with underlying hatred. Upon leaving the shop, the women rushed toward their estate. Their state of hurry didn't thwart them from audibly rebuking the outfit of every passerby.

Intentionally falling behind, Hope silently observed the women's behavior.

"Once he sets eyes on your beautiful gowns, he'll be entranced. Without a doubt, the bevy of mediocre women in this town will pale in comparison." Mrs. Bonnet didn't care a bit that anyone passing might hear her words, for she knew her daughters would soon be upper crust. "Especially when he lays eyes on you, my perfectly crafted Grace," she declared. The girls' eagerness to flaunt their new purchases overcame them as they waited for the chance to get acquainted with the fresh suitor. People are like ants, following whatever golden crumb drops to the desolate ground, and in their greedy attempt to devour every treasure, the foot of humanity crushes them. Their voracity for material wealth inevitably causes an abrupt ending to their life. I am at the foot of society. The ant crusher. I decide when people live or die. I have the power to end selfish acts and clear the world of greed, squashing all forms of corruption. One by one, I will fulfill my vow to Father, starting with the Bonnet dames, for they were ever so pretty to me.

Four

DYING TO KILL

A euphoric urge ran through my body as I realized tonight was the big night! The very eve Father had groomed me for. Years of dreams and visions haunted my nights, training me for a prodigious battle. Like a soldier going to war, I was equipped to begin my gruesome crusade of cleansing the town of its most wretched refuse. With great elation, I stood up and proclaimed that it was time to meet the grand Bonnet sisters, the most desirable bodies in the land, trophies any like-minded crusader would revel in the opportunity to put on display. I imagined their bodies and minds were able to cleanse my soul with every ounce of their bloody tears. Do not allow your envy to overtake your admiration of me; I have only gained my status by being one lucky bastard. Keep faith--the glorious thing about luck is that it does not rely upon social boundaries, allowing everyone the opportunity to experience its graces.

Father had selected today as the day I would choose a wife. I drifted in vivid thoughts surrounding the forthcoming events. Suddenly I awoke from my trancelike state to find myself dressed and standing on the bottom step of my grand stairwell. I approached the main entrance of my estate and took three spectacular steps outside the large archway. As I stood admiring the grounds from my entry steps, three knocks echoed behind me. "Sounds like Father approves," I murmured. It was as if he had wished me luck! With this sign of his agreement, a newfound twinkle formed in my eye. The love I received from Father differed from anything I had ever experienced, and his irrevocable belief in my ability to succeed left no option for failure.

I looked dashing, and as a well-groomed prospect, I didn't have a single doubt I could swoon the hardest of hearts. My resolve intensified as I noticed Father's dark blanket surround my spirit and infuse warmth into my being. Upon the merging of our essences, our breaths grew steady with the synchronization of our heartbeats. Intensity and excitement continued to breed as I approached the carriage that would take me to my destination. My pace escalated as I realized I must not be late for my much-anticipated arrival. As I neared what I like to refer to as my "chariot to hell," a dim red halo was visible, blithely floating above the coach's wooden walls. The interior was barely visible through the curtained side window because of the darkness of the cabin. I raised my hand to hail attention from the driver's seat, and to my disbelief, no one came to my service. The carriage did not budge; not a soul came to open my door. My eyes floated from the driver's seat to the carriage's storage compartment, and a grand realization came to mind. "Oh, fuck!" I spewed, my face red with an angry comprehension. As if I were snapping to from a case of amnesia, the imagery of the previous night rushed back to me. Without a driver, I would have no way of being delivered to my destination with chauffeured panache.

An irrepressible emotion took over my body: fury resonated through my core as the memories of my arrival flashed back in evocative sequences, tarnishing my jovial mind with reality. "Damn you!" I shouted. "Damn, damn, damn you, selfish bastard!" I shouted in frustration as I glanced at the back of the carriage. Quite inconvenienced, I crossly dashed to the rear storage compartment and opened it. As the lid parted ways with its dark cavernous counterpart, I found myself met with the old man's hollow eyes. It stunned me that even in death he looked unequivocally repulsive. My astonishment forced me to study his carcass more closely. I gazed into his open right eye, examining its increased concavity. The eyeball floated in what appeared to be an ill-fitting encasement. My view panned to the edges of the velvet-lined compartment to see that he still lay as placed: a heap of shit. My eyes grazed his feet but dashed back to his pupils, which continued to stare at me. Death's glare emanated from his recessed sockets while the robust smells of rotting flesh tingled my eyes to the point of watering.

What would the Bonnets think if this chariot of stench rolled up to my future bride's home? Nothing is more irksome than an inconvenience and being forced to acknowledge the old man's pointless presence created an excessive inconvenience. "That's it!" I exclaimed to the beat of my gloved hand's impressive clap. The aroma no longer maddened my delicate nasal passages, instead transitioning to a pleasant fragrance one could associate with new beginnings. "Snap out of it!" I murmured as I tapped the side of my head, inundated with recollections of the man's revolting character. My body shivered and my teeth clenched as I recalled my reasons for finding him repugnant. Instantly, adrenaline rushed through my veins, and a soothing ease spiked my blood.

The flash of emotions solidified my comprehension; I was in my element. Father's presence continued to magnify at a rate that aligned with the tempo of my metamorphosis. His existence supplied my essence; I owed nothing short of my life to him. Though it was impossible to repay Father for all he laid at my feet, I did my best to follow his will and solidify his pride each day. In his honor, I had to conquer each societal ideal that threatened the ruination of future generations.

With Father's quiet guidance, I turned my attention back to the carcass. I leaned in closer, glancing at the lifeless body. Nothing appeared different to me; his stare continued to challenge my tolerance. Poking his eye proved tempting because of its appearance. The pressure caused the white to moisten with bodily fluids that one might misinterpret as tears. He looked peaceful, however, neither dead nor alive. I grabbed his oil-stained shirt, coating my hand with fetid juices produced by his filthy presence. Fervently I shook his being from my fingertips. Suddenly I understood why he looked so peaceful in his velvet-lined accommodations; Father was to blame.

His fixated eyes revealed the truth: Father had renewed his life by inhabiting the decaying capsule. He had handed the nameless man a new identity, thus allowing him undeserving peace. I never knew death could be so spectacular until I encountered this weary moment of calm. A flare of anger rushed through my limbs as I snapped back to the sad realization that my carriage was no longer available for my visit to my potential brides. "Why!" I shouted at the carriage's regal shadow. With a new sense of urgency, I paced back and forth, back and forth. Then an idea sparked my mind!

Without a second thought, I reached into the compartment, snatched the corpse by the tattered coat collar, and tossed the human trash violently to the cold and unforgiving cobblestone. Again, I grabbed a handful of the collar and dragged the carcass up to the estate's entrance, where I placed the paralyzed body inside the entryway, out of view from busybodies. Once it was obscured, I took a moment to gather my thoughts. Looking from side to side, I glimpsed my statuesque reflection, which stopped me steadfast in my tracks. I almost had forgotten about the mirror in the foyer. "How could any woman resist such a handsome creature?" I cooed as I looked deep into my loveless eyes. Impressed with my appearance after the exasperating altercation with the carcass, I smoothed my tousled black hair and adjusted my imported black silk coat. As I stared at my reflection, giddy with disbelief over my perfection, I looked more debonair than ever.

It was as if the corpse had given me a more youthful appearance. "Amazing," I whispered under my breath. The old man I once reviled now garnered my gratitude for providing me with enhanced youthful attractiveness. He had sacrificed his soul for the greater good, and for his sacrifice, a show of appreciation was called for. After all, who wants to live with an enemy in their cheerful hands? Not me, for I want a friend, not a foe. Smiling, I tipped the brim of my hat to the mangled man. I then locked the doors and carried on my merry way. Whistling sounds, mirroring the notes of a concert pianist caressing a piano's iridescent keys, emerged through my impeccably straight teeth. As I strode toward the carriage, the whistle grew louder as it left my plump lips, and a joyous pep infused my steps. I was a newfound man. I danced across the cobblestone path as trumpets of triumph sounded through the evening air.

Nothing would stop me from playing my brass chorus of merry thoughts as I set out to meet my perfect matches. As I analyzed the deficient driver's carriage, I had to reconsider my means of transportation yet again. I devised a fresh plan with haste while eyeing the two noble steeds harnessed to the front of the carriage. I unharnessed the more impressive stallion and grabbed a saddle and bridle from the driver's seat compartment. Once the steed was saddled, I mounted it and rode into the afternoon. What is nobler than a fine-looking man on a robust stallion? Arriving as a knight in shining armor to the Bonnets' estate was the perfect choice for this special occasion. It excited me to imagine their reactions when they caught their first glance at my tall, dark figure mounted on the back of this fine beast. My dominance and masculinity would make them quiver to their core. The steed's gait was smooth, making the travel time seem but a moment. Forthrightly at my destination, I slowed the horse's pace and leisurely passed through the property's gates. As I made my way down the cobblestone path, I analyzed the Bonnet estate.

I will not bore you with tedious details such as house color. The exterior was mediocre compared to mine, and that is the only detail worth mentioning. Observing beyond the bland architecture and assessing the finer points of the house itself, I noticed a figure stationed at a window on the main floor. Its face stared into this chosen soul and looked shy of sixteen, with delicate features that resembled those of a baby hen. Though pale in appearance overall, she looked well maintained and prideful. If put on the matrimonial auction block, she would gather a pretty penny for her looks. I did not know what words would stream from her fledgling mouth, but from her outward appearance, she possessed every ideal attribute. She had rich blond hair pulled on top of her head, with curls veering down from her scalp to her temples. Her wide blue eyes resembled the purest of oceans. Although her features were sharp, they still appeared soft and mystical. Their structural presence no doubt kept any man lingering on her every word, regardless of the verbiage, quality, or content. I must admit her face was quite entrancing. Our eyes locked in an exchange, causing her to realize I had caught her gawping at my arrival. Out of mortification, she coyly scampered away from the window. By her conduct, it was obvious Mr. and Mrs. Bonnet had not disciplined her when she was a child. A proper young lady would never covertly observe a guest. From her appearance, I gathered she must be the youngest daughter, the one answering to the name "Grace." *My pleasure to meet you,* I thought with childlike excitement.

The stallion's coat shone like a newly forged blade as its shoes clicked across the cold stones. Its pace slowed even further as I approached the estate's entrance. Again, I surveyed the estate, noting the exits. Next to the front porch, a lamppost stood guard. Although the sky was not yet dim enough for the light to share its shine, it remained a fixed staring eye. The light lacked the control to stand still, and I wondered what knowledge the glowing flame was privy to. Would you not wonder what every person in the town was up to? I saw the light once again with a grimace and a lingering glare. *Just wait,* I mused. *The eye will be so delighted when I purge the town's pollution from its spectacle lens.* We would work together, to provide a new beginning for the settlement.

After tying the steed to the post, I began my magnificent entrance. A rush of warmth entered my body and caressed my every toe, brushed my leg, and crept up my thigh. Giddiness overtook me as I approached the estate's terrace, my cane leading my every move as I carried myself with inherent pride. I was irresistible and dapper to a level that neither man nor woman could resist my temptation. I am not abashed to admit I exalt myself regarding my appearance. Anyone with my extraordinary features should be nothing but arrogant. Like a fighting cock ready for a brawl, I was eager to engage in an altercation. Trust me when I say I am aware of what society considers as good looks, and mine can be classified as desirable. Let me let you in on a small disclosure: not even the wine-drinking whore I slaughtered, or my intended awaiting inside the forsaken estate, would ever know what you are about to learn. Eureka, I have a secret plan that provides all in this cold estate an opportunity to take part in the dwindling of their desires and the eradication of their ambitions. They would submit to my every whim. Traditional courting is a waste of time; I favor a more blatant approach, which includes placing a parting kiss on the lips so they will never forget my presence. The skill with which I delivered this kiss would assure fireworks displays in their minds long after my farewell, leaving them in unforgettable bliss.

Only after I forced myself to end my scheming trance did I realize I had made it to the estate's large metal double entry. The Bonnets had unnecessarily encrusted the left doorway with a sizable family seal painted in silver tones. The image implied I would receive my full money's worth beyond the gate. I raised my coiled fist to the excessively over-adorned silver-shilling pomposity. The gratuitous ornate brass-and-silver detail aided as an effective distraction to shield the Bonnets' hidden secrets. My hand did not even complete its first knock before a withered face appeared, meeting my question-filled gaze. Without a moment given to comprehend the face that broke my train of thought, the decrepit lips of the woman spoke. "Good afternoon. Follow me," the antiquated maid discharged from her mouth with ease. Standing no taller than my shoulders, the shriveled creature was hunched, with facial features that rivaled those of ancient elephants. The dress the Bonnets had provided for her was snug, high necked, and shit brown in color. One might think the owners of an estate would take pride in properly dressing the first creature their guests encountered, but by the looks of it, I would ascertain they had run out of money. I gave her a long, stern scowl before deciding to follow. Who was she to not allow my knocking? Did she think of herself as the gatekeeper of my destiny? Maybe her disconcerting nature was a mere manifestation of my greatest fear. Or she was nothing more than an emotionless demon born to be a valuable pawn in the family's miserable fate?

Without a doubt, she was most surely a demon! I had no question of my assertion; she had robbed me of my ritual, thus jeopardizing my good luck. She would never guess the frightful monster she had aided in unleashing. Before entering a residence, I always favored knocking in threes and habitually did this twice through. After the knocks, I adjusted my lapel and invited Father to join me. Why such a pattern? Let me educate you, as the answer is quite simple: it brings me comfort and peace. Many have queried me about this. I chuckle at the thought of the question, for what is three plus three? Any juvenile can answer the simple equation. If you guessed six, then bravo to you, for that is my favorite number. Father came to me as a shadow on the sixth day of the six month at the sixth hour and showed me a life I never imagined possible. Do not view Father's actions as charity, for he blessed me with esteemed status and the utmost attractiveness for a greater purpose, transforming me into an angel called on to save the soul of society. On that day I gained both a father and an irreplaceable voice of reason. Father had ordained me to rid the world of filthy cattle that hide behind "honorable" facades. As I returned to the present, I realized the leather-faced peppery-haired woman was leading me down a long hallway littered with distasteful artwork, on a straight path to face my destiny.

Upon entering a room at the end of the hall, I unclenched my jaw, released my tight grip on my stick of gold, and tipped my hat toward the hag. "Much obliged," I told the maid with closed teeth. I was barely able to squeeze the well-mannered words through my clasped lips. Moving with a swagger, I followed the creature to another door inside the room we had just entered. This entry seemed to be less eccentric, as if they'd spent a considerable sum of money decorating the outside entrance of the estate rather than finishing the home's interior, intending to give the impression that it was grand through and through. I concluded that estates match the people who dwell within the walls because, like the estates, they too try to mask their true identities with gross materialistic display. From the corner of my view, I caught the hatchet-faced woman looking at me with her beady eyes. I believe the housekeeper reflects a family's position more than the riches they wear; that they had a dilapidated, unpleasant maid solidified my analogy. The unnerving woman and disruptor of my ritual were so unbearable to look at that I was forced to look above her head and pretend to admire the cheap reprinted artwork crookedly hanging on the walls. Out of my peripheral vision, I noticed her raise her scarred burnt finger and point toward a room. "This way," she said. Her gravelly, cracking voice was so annoying and unpleasant that if a flock of birds heard it their organs would spontaneously eviscerate, and each body would tumble from the clear blue sky. She hobbled ahead of me and opened the bland wooden door.

I no longer needed to acknowledge her, for she had fulfilled her purpose. I moved past her wrinkly corpse to the parlor, where the three sisters stood, with Mrs. Bonnet behind them. Lined up like cows up for auction, the sisters stared at me with creeping eyes filled with fiery lust, confirming their seductive intent. Promptly upon my arrival, Mr. Bonnet approached me from the edge of the parlor. This was a very rare sighting indeed, for few have seen the man in person. His alcoholic stupor seemed to have won his daily battle in his choice between facing his miserable life with sobriety or drunkenness. He moved toward me at a sluggish pace for his age--so slowly, in fact, that I began analyzing his facial structure, counting his wrinkles just like one would measure the rings of an oak tree's stump to determine its age. I noticed he had dressed up for the occasion by wearing what looked like the attire from his wedding day. Although at one point in his ghastly life the tweed suit had been sharp, it now clung to his body and showcased his belly, which undoubtedly was full of whiskey. The stain I spotted on his right lapel became the highlight of his existence. Although people believed he had money, he dressed as though he had not a pot to piss in.

Maybe this was not Mr. Bonnet but a debauched impostor. What an embarrassing piece of flesh! His fraudulent entity smelled worse than his alcoholic sweat. This initial encounter is why I will forever think of him as the impostor of the Bonnets. The cows in this house had sucked both his money and soul dry. He took so long to cross the room that I wanted to give him a round of applause when he shook my hand. The pleasant atmosphere was short-lived, as his repulsive stench of copious liquor and week-old cologne hit my mouth. The odor of rotten flesh was less offensive.

If they forced me to spend a day walking in his broken-down shoes with four leeches biting at my back, I too would drink my life away. He should have kissed the ground I walked on, for I would help him end this infestation of problematic leeches that sucked the very blood from his life. I would have liked nothing more than to tell him to lay off the booze, for his sorrows would soon resolve. Sadly, for him, my calling must remain a secret for now. If only he knew my purpose, he would thank me for making his life bearable again. The thought caused me to smile. "I present to you my three daughters, Grace, Eve, and Hope," the disheveled man said as he pointed across the room. I noticed he mentioned the youngest daughter first as if trying to market his most-prized pig. Scanning the girls from left to right, I noted their forged smiles were consistent. At first glance, I realized my earlier assertions had been correct. The young woman I had spotted in the estate's window upon my arrival was, in fact, the youngest daughter. Attempting to steal my heart, she had chosen to dress herself in a soft-blue empire gown with matching feathers placed in her perfectly spiraled ringlets. The timorous persona exhibited ten minutes prior was now void, her true self-present. She obviously garnered attention from potential mates through her strategic display of naivete. Her eye batting and ankle-exposing dress adjustments would catch the eyes of the most eager suitors. I found it entertaining to watch as she tried to get my eyes glued to her. If only she knew the attention she was seeking would be her last. I scanned the three daughters again, my glance falling on the neutral middle girl, Eve. She had dirty-blond hair and light muddy brown eyes. The dress that draped her body was a subtle yellow with off-white lace. Although she did not look as pure as Grace, she still cast a subtle charm. It was obvious the middle child had just as much self-confidence as Grace but a less delightful appearance to support the attainment of her desires. Her eagerness to converse with me was obvious, for she did not stop biting her lip and lustfully gawking. The expression in her eyes read like that of a prostitute and reminded me of my first kill, the redheaded wench. Eve looked me up and down, showing no sign of self-respect or dignified restraint.

As my eyes skimmed over the three girls for the third and final time, I met the gaze of the eldest daughter, Hope. She carried herself in a way that exhibited her "loving family" had made her quite aware she was the plainest, most undesirable of the three. The way she was appareled made the disparaging treatment quite apparent. Clearly not caring whether she espoused an honorable man, Mrs. Bonnet had dressed her in a color scheme like that of the maid. Hope's features were more pointed but not appealingly. I would liken her resemblance to that of a rodent-hunting falcon. She wore an expression of constant agony, a look that reminded me of my past self before Father had rescued me from my distress. A story lay hidden behind her troubled eyes, but I would not be the one to uncover it. Hope's eyes were dark; in fact, they were the darkest shade of black I had ever seen. Just a moment of looking into them gave me a sense of asphyxiation. I don't know if the darkness came from her soul or if it was the endless disdain toward her family exuding from her being.

As I looked over the girls' heads, I briefly made eye contact with Mrs. Bonnet. The wretched woman didn't try to hide her prejudice regarding which daughter she favored. She wore a similar blue dress and had made an unsuccessful attempt to curl her hair in ringlets to match. Within her wilted curls sat an assortment of secondhand feathers. Gaudily colored makeup resembling splatters of bird shit covered her face. In no way did any of her pathetic efforts match Grace's perfectly cloaked body, perfectly quaffed hair, and porcelain skin. I had no interest in learning about her or digesting a single word she spewed. Being forced to look at her filled me with rage and tempted me to expel vile sputum at her feet. Have you heard of this adage before? A man's personality will attract a woman's hidden charm. Well, I have, and it is true, so I will refrain from showing my anger at this moment. To win the race, I must remain grounded.

The whores made an impressive spectacle of themselves. They had primped and propped up every asset just for my viewing. Turning toward Mr.

Bonnet, I declared, "Thank you, kind sir, for your gracious hospitality." I kept my emotions veiled to allow my intentions to remain a mystery. I requested Mr. Bonnet to briefly distance himself from the herd, away from inquisitive ears. The motive was obvious, for I was revealing my selection. Once we were out of sight from the cattle, I leaned in close to his hair-filled ear and whispered, "Would it be acceptable to take the youngest Bonnet for a stroll around the courtyard?" As the words left my lips, his booze-enriched pupils lit up. With the reflexes of a rabbit, Mr. Bonnet jolted his hand forward and immediately summoned Grace to approach. Smugly she straightened her dress and glanced at her two elder sisters boastfully. She knew she was about to be the prodigious recipient of the lone prize. As she walked toward me, she developed a vivacity that overtook each step, causing her blue dress to wave from side to side as she attempted to wiggle her hips back and forth. This was a motion her body could not carry out because she lacked the voluptuous assets necessary for such movement.

As she approached, I did the gentlemanly thing and held out my arm to aid her capable body. Through this trivial action, she was consumed with admiration. She seized my elbow so ravenously that I thought she would surely rip it out of my bony socket. The sureness of her actions left no question that I preferred her and that she held probable future ownership over my bank account. She proceeded to walk next to me as though she had won a pageant. *Stupid girl!* I thought. *If only she knew the grim prize she just won.* With haste, we stepped outside to take our stroll. I led the walk because a man should always be one step ahead of the woman-- especially one he might claim ownership of after matrimony. The irrelevant talk that accompanied the walk was predictable and quite useless, with Grace sharing few words that sang a single note of intelligence. What made her fundamental nature even more maddening was her shrill, giddy, childish laugh. Her laughter was so high-pitched that any man's eardrums would bleed upon hearing a single titter. You may wonder why I selected Grace if I found her so repulsive. I chose the sheep, the one conditioned to fulfill any command. Through her actions, she clarified she would do anything to be one step above her sisters. Out of all the daughters, it was obvious she was the rottenest apple and the easiest target. She was the perfect first choice.

Our steps grew quieter as the cobblestones transitioned to a dirt path that led to the courtyard's center. Scanning the terrain, I spotted a perfect bench to take a seat. As my eyes fixated on the location, I picked up my pace, forcing Grace to walk more quickly. I motioned for her to set down, emphasizing my firmness to make her comfortable. Nothing was more important than for my strategy to continue without disruption. As I stared into her soul, I glimpsed Father's shadowy reflection in her eyes; I could have sworn they were blue upon our first meeting, but now they had turned a shade of red. Her pheromones were so unbearable they made my head hurt. She reeked of horrible thoughts and pretentious feelings. Despite my discomfort, I had prepared for this moment for months through my thoughts, dreams, and Father's sound guidance. Earlier that day, in my drawing room, I had written a masterpiece of a letter with Father's insightful help. He is perfectly clever. I had tucked away this letter in my right coat pocket. It would prove to be the catalyst for the successful implementation of my endeavor.

The location's tranquility allowed me to open my mind and listen to all the voices dancing in my head. Like a soft gust of wind, they guided my thoughts and actions as they stirred through me. Directed by encouragement from Father, I reached into my pocket. As I touched the paper, a light of excitement moved through Grace's face. It was as though she had expected me to pull a large diamond ring from my coat and propose an offer of marriage. In her mind, a proposal would make her the sure winner.

When I removed my hand from my pocket and presented the letter, she gazed at me with a bit of disappointment. "You are the most beautiful woman I have ever laid eyes upon. I can't imagine living my life without you," I declared with a bit of fire hidden in my smile. I knew I was irresistible, for Father had made me so. The light breeze caressing my hair and the exquisite lighting of my masculine features made me most desirable and unattainable. The day's timing was perfect. Nothing made me happier than to have power over others.

The quiet garden supplied the perfect setting to further lure her into my trap. After I explained that my family had left me as the sole heir of a hefty fortune, I detailed my extensive list of assets. Grace's eyes lit up at the grandiose picture. She seemed most excited about my magnificent estate, where she would live as the headmistress. "We will fill your sisters with envy till the day they perish, for I will pamper you with the finest of riches." As the magical words left my tongue, Grace's eyes grew so expansive with greed that I thought they would pop.

I now knew it would be impossible for her to turn down any invitation I offered. Her gullibility surpassed her stupidity. I found I didn't even have to carry the conversation further to engage her interest. She required no extra additives or descriptors to entice her. I laid the letter in her palm and looked deep into her fire-glazed eyes. "*No one* must know about this; your reputation and mine would be at significant risk," I said, then asked her to nod to confirm she understood. I explained to her that many individuals had tried to threaten my inheritance out of jealousy. For this reason, I told her we would need to elope. The story smelled of horseshit, but to Grace, it was pure romance. Her eyes displayed a shallow understanding as she profusely nodded. With each of her fate-sealing head bobs, I grinned at the fact that I knew my plan was in motion. To think her daylight would soon be extinguished and mine would shine only brighter. She snatched the letter from me and tucked it away in her dress's bodice. With promises in place, we rose to our feet, and I led her back to the estate's interior. The return of her to her bibulous Father could not happen fast enough. Immediately upon entering the room, Grace gave her family a look of social elevation and sat down haughtily. As she did so, her mother made her contentment known by giving her a slight nudge of approval. Not wanting to ruin their moment of celebration, I said a brief farewell and swooped out of their prison into a gust of shadows. Overcome with my gallant success, I fled into the fading light.

Five

THE LETTER

Notes are quite an unconventional means of communication. One crumple and the light from a single match can erase the words from memory. Are you still thinking about the note I passed to Grace in the garden? If you answered "yes," it is understandable. Let me assure you I am dwelling on that piece of papyrus as well. Each quill stroke on the paper painted a path toward greatness. We will soon reminisce about that detail together, but I dare not stop my thoughts for the moment. Are you still anxious about what lies beneath the twine and seal of the letter? Curiosity will not kill the cat unless the greedy cat fails to uncover an answer that never was meant to be private. I will save you angst and spill the tea of wondering minds into your cup.

Many have said the presentation is the most crucial part of a show or performance. Some also argue that a great deal of significance lies in how the viewer judges the content because first impressions can be everything. I believe the most critical factor will forever be the reader's state of mind. If struggling or incompetent, the individual comprehending the words will have a skewed interpretation of any message's contents. A stupid interpreter has no hope at all when deciphering the simplest of scribbles. Now I know what you are thinking: why have I still not disclosed what was within this letter? I must overwhelm you with suspense, the gripping anticipation so grand that it could swell a heart to the point of bursting. The sweat dripping from your forehead is not cause for concern. Rest assured that my words stand ready to lick the droplets of your baited anticipation. Without further ado, I answer the burning question "What words did the note to poor Grace contain?"

My reason for picking the youngest girl as my first victim was straightforward. When I saw her age and her avaricious eyes, I immediately knew she had something to prove. Whether it stemmed from her fresh foray into the courting process or her promiscuous core, I knew I would sway her. Her obnoxious personality made it uncomplicated for me to make my first selection, for she was the most willing patient in my quest to cure society's disease. Now to the letter: I invited her to my private quarters while making my intentions seem nowhere near desperate. To give her the impression she still needed to work for my affection, I inserted a few stipulations she needed to follow. As she was used to following her parents' rubrics, I decided the conditional portion of this ruse would come as an act of familiarity. The subsequent details are a condensed version of the most critical instructions in the note. First, I requested her to leave her estate amid the blackest cover of night so no one would catch sight of her and notice our improprieties. She would view this step as a caring gesture, but for me, it provided collateral. The timing of her departure not only was wise but also reflected a sympathetic concern for Grace's reputation. Let me state, for all to hear, that I am one of the few respectable gentlemen left in the world. Before anyone would question her unexpected disappearance, I would need to create an alibi. The last thing I wanted was for the Bonnet family to assume mischief was at play. I do not wish for a babbling trail of bimbos pointing in my ambiguous direction. All of us know my intentions only have her utmost interests in mind. In the message, I clarified I was on her side. In addition, I expressed she would have all she ever wanted, including a magnificent ring, upon her arrival at my home, to prove her worth. Understanding the young cow's true personality, I knew soliciting a marriage proposal would lead her anywhere of my choosing. A good deal of you may question my predictions and think, *What if she isn't vulnerable?* Let me explain my evaluation; I realized her personality when I stared into the darkened sockets that led to her soul. From the moment I saw her peer through the curtain-covered windows, I knew she was a gift to me from Father himself. He bestowed her presence upon me and has never led me astray. Father knew society would be far grander without Grace's selfish primped carcass taking up space, and I was obliged to perform the honorable duty.

After I gave Grace the message and departed from the residence, a frantic preparatory swiftness ensued. With prodigious comprehension, I tucked the plan away into my mind. I apologize if you feel shortchanged because of your limited story preview, but I have little time to waste because of the preparations required for the story's continuation. To be honest, I relish the fact that I left you on your seat's edge or the "edge of your seat," as some might say. I hope to God that your ass is plump, for I would hate a bruise to appear on your rump or a blood clot to form in your sedentary legs. Trust me, the numb limbs will be worth the salacious conversational assets you will gain from witnessing this tale. From the moment I handed Grace the letter, my every move became timed to a clockwork beat. My departure was seamless, and excitement mounted with new beginnings in sight.

A foreign sound resonated in my chest; one I liken to that of a lifeless fetus in a womb regaining a heartbeat. I can get carried away on this subject, but time is of the essence, so I will spare you the extensive verbiage and provide an estimated timeline of the evening's events following the letter's passing. I use the term "estimated timeline" because I do not want you to lose faith in my prestigious time-sensitive nature if the schedule varies by a mere second. If you could not take my words as facts, in whom could you put your faith? The thought of imprecise timetables crossing my mind was distressing. Six minutes after I left the Bonnet estate, Grace returned to her bedroom quarters only to retrieve the heartfelt letter from her bosom. She was enthralled that a suitor had thrust a romantic note upon her. She would have one hour after the clock struck six till dusk revealed its dimming veil and a decision had to be made. From the moment twilight filled the earth's sky, Grace would have one hour before her glorious rebirth. The moment she arrived at my estate, darkness would flood every street corner and slay every fleck of hope-filled light.

Do you believe the calculations of time are mere coincidence? For those of you still choosing to follow along, tell me, how many minutes are in an hour? If you find the analysis too complex, there is no need to strain your mind, dear friends. I will gladly hand you the answer. There are sixty minutes in one hour. So which number is prevalent within my plan's time constraints? If you guessed six--yes, lucky six--you are correct! Bravo for not being a complete idiot. Give yourself a pat on the back and revel in your sense of pitiable accomplishment. The number six provides a steady reminder that Father graces my life with kindness. My life's alignment with this devilish number assures I am on the right path, and the sense of calmness provided by the consistent use of this number engulfs me.

As I lingered in a faint shadow cast from a nearby tree, I heard small children singing. The harmonic voices initially lifted my ghoulish spirit and calmed my clamoring ears until the music grew louder than the rushes of air traversing the sky. I liken it to the sound of a cargo ship hitting a port. To the left of the maple tree that stood next to my estate, a great shadow was cast by the skies transitioning light reflecting off the useless carriage. The shadow grew with a wave of solidarity, joining me as I headed toward hell. The estate seemed lifeless, not a sound of a human breath or the sign of a burning lantern embellishing the place. After dismounting and tying the agitated steed to the tree, I gave his long coal-black mane a tug and made my way to the entry of my estate. Did I mention how much grander my wealth stood compared to that of the other male prospects in Northburry? Once I reached the ornate entrance, I unlocked it and let myself in. I did not perform my ritualistic knocks.

As I stood in the foyer, I closed my eyes and took in a profound lungful of air, certain it would show my appreciation for all that Father had given me. After the large inhalation, I gasped. "Smells like shit!" Tracing the repulsive odor, I noticed the smell of excrement was emanating from the carriage driver I had placed in the foyer before my jaunt to the Bonnets. I glanced at my feet to see his limb sticking out, as if trying to wave and welcome me home. "No, no, little piggy." I chuckled as I kicked his arm. "This will not do." Staring at the decaying corpse, I snatched him by his crooked feet and dragged him toward the coat closet, depositing his sloughing carcass just outside the small accommodation. The airtight door appeared perfect for concealment, including his unmistakable aroma. Here the odor would indeed remain unnoticed. Please know I consider myself a tidy person, and this task is just a tiny sampling of spring-cleaning skills.

I scowled at the corpse's new position, for he looked too comfortable. Once again, I tightened my grip around his distorted feet. "Let's celebrate my guests' arrival, grand sir," I heckled the stiff body, whose face had turned blackish blue. With his feet caught in my spiderlike clutch, I swung his body from side to side, stroking the floor in a sweeping motion. The body oscillated across the wooden planks, resembling a filthy yarn mop scrubbing vomit from a tavern floor. Giddy squeals of delight filled my gut as I realized I had discovered an invention. As his dead weight swished around, his sticky cranium and greasy, stringy curls picked up the filth from the floorboards. Although the concept is unconventional, I might be on to something. "With a large house comes countless responsibilities," I said, as I could not help wonder why I had not hired a maid yet. I hummed a merry tune, the notes resonating with my spring cleaning. With each gleeful stroke, my blood rushed, and my thoughts switched to overdrive. Finishing the floor's new shine, I dragged the dust-coated corpse toward the inexplicably wide-open closet. The peculiarity of the opened door caused me to assume Father was behind the inviting welcome. Within the cozy nook, I observed a layer of darkness. It was unmistakable that the hospitable opacity inhabiting the cozy space wanted Father for himself. The closet's darkness emanated a hollow sense of desire and desperation. My excitement grew with the thought of sharing my every conquest with Father and further garnering his pride. Driven by the urge to expedite the carriage driver's move to his new accommodations, I employed a bit more rapidity toward his relocation. As I inched closer to the darkness, my blood boiled and flesh burned. I stuffed his body inside and slammed the door behind him. It was the perfect location for him to get a much-deserved rest after his maid-related duties. I knocked six times on the closet's wooden seal and stepped away, leaving the carriage driver to his beauty sleep.

I must admit I had developed a bit of a liking for my companion and acknowledge a sense of yearning for the camaraderie of my closet-bound friend. To distract me from my debilitating thoughts, I waltzed to the parlor and took a seat on my beloved chair. The magnificent chair I speak of had been bestowed upon me to serve as my throne of inspiration. Each devious plan I would develop in Northburry would transpire while I was seated on its superbly tacked, down-filled fabric. It was the only seat that provided me relaxation and allowed me to produce intelligent, raucous banter for my daily debates with Father. I enjoyed Father's shadow, which bellowed to me and reaped all deserving sorrows derived from our company. My parlor was meticulous, and I found its structured appearance quaint and perfect for ensuring productivity. A sense of homey comfort embraced my body as my eyes frantically searched each musty corner for Father's presence. His existence always prevailed where each wall merged with another. Whenever direction was needed, I would be seated alone, staring at each seam, awaiting Father's guidance. My focused solitude helped Father appear in my moments of need. You may investigate the corners of your home at night, wondering if you are as fortunate as me, and see the father I speak of. Let me be clear: I am the only one endowed with the gift of seeing Father's shadow; I am the chosen one.

A single piece of furniture shared the room with my favorite chair and was positioned in the center of my cozy parlor: a solid oak desk with cherry trim, hand-carved from trees harvested in spring. They cut the trees in a manner that allowed vinelike branches to remain woven through every ledge and leg of the masterpiece. Like me, each component embodies a mystifying attribute. Entranced observers overlook the dangerous warning signs of my twisted branches and, like flies to honey, the complexity and beauty lures them to unsuspecting terrors. They approach the rarity with hyper-focused entrancement only to find the concealed thorns after their flesh is pricked. As blood drips from the wound, a shocking realization of their circumstance occurs. The critical difference between the thorn-filled vine and myself is that I disdain messes. The avoidance of blood being spilled is imperative; I prefer to leave no residue for any to witness. It is unsophisticated, barbaric, and a rather large libido suppressant. A quill pen and sheet of papyrus lay positioned in the center of my desk, awaiting my arrival. I remained prepared to document Father's bidding and worldly advice, as I never knew when he would bless me with his wisdom.

Across from my desk hung a long, oval looking glass. I assured I positioned the mirror at eye level so whether sitting or standing at my writing table, I did not have to part ways from my impeccable reflection. Why hang a mirror where I can gaze into my own eyes? I chose to have a mirror hanging in each room, so I could view my flawless appearance every second of every day. When coming and going from my chair and entering and leaving each room, I wished to see only my attractiveness. Observing myself in reflective glass is quite fulfilling. To be frank, who wouldn't want to look at me? I laughed at the thought of someone never experiencing a view of my masculine beauty.

I cannot garner enough admiration for my appearance. In fact, when I expire, rather than being placed in a grand mausoleum, I would prefer that a world-renowned butcher cut each crowning feature from my body and preserve it in jars of formaldehyde for all to marvel. Then and only then will my legacy of beauty find use as a teaching tool for youth to learn what physical perfection should look like. From my chiseled jawline to my striking dark features, I will always be considered the "man of irreplaceable perfection." A title only I deserve.

I found great pleasure sitting in my chair in the unlit room, alone with my mirror. My typical facial structure, enhanced by daylight, was now replaced with one amplified by the room's shadows. Only one distinctive feature remained in the mirror's reflection: the exaggerated whites of my entrancing eyes. As I stared into my orbs, I pondered my life and the work I was to achieve.

I speculated whether the last moments of my victims resembled what an antelope experiences when stalked by a ravenous lion. Do living creatures perceive a sense of terror before the chase, or do they live a life of naivete with little anxiety? Like the lion, I am a respected predator, stalking my prey and premeditating my attacks, preparing my strategy so my whore-slaying pounce is rehearsed. Though similar, I am more dangerous than the majestic beast, for I have Father behind me.

Tight black upholstery adorned with six red cloth buttons enveloped my beloved chair. The same colors and button patterns were identifiable throughout the estate. Extra buttons and fabric were stowed away for safekeeping, assuring the decorative style remained consistent. Analyzing all buttons more closely than usual, I realized each one now appeared like a small pool of blood. The vision created a vicious urge in me to attack any living thing that entered my lair. I crouched as low as the floor's shadows, camouflaged only by my chair. "I am a lion," I whispered as I cocked my head back, looking at the ceiling and letting out a guttural roar. Regaining my composure, I awaited my prey.

Each corner of the parlor had six stained-glass windows arranged in a symmetrical pattern. It might sound simple but let me provide a bit more detail regarding their placement. Every window cluster rested in groups of three, shaped like a pyramid. Why a pyramid? The peak of the pyramid represents the elevated position of the lead hunter in the bestial pecking order. I am the peak, the top predator of life's hierarchical food chain. My station commands me to purge the weak and release them from their misery on this earth. While pondering the animal kingdom, I caught a glimpse through the stained glass and noticed the sun had almost completely departed. My smirk widened as I realized someone would soon invite my inner lion to come out to play. The last sliver of sun peered through the clear glass shards. The orange light condensed, causing it to enter the room in blood-red tones, showing solidarity with the ruminations in my mind.

Embracing the red light against my skin, I took a moment to collect my thoughts. *How should I take care of the demon that will arrive tonight?* I asked myself as scenarios regarding how my night would unravel raced through my head. My favorite thought of all was how it would end. "No, no, no, this is all wrong!" I yelled. The handsome man looking back at me from the mirror's reflection calmed my aggressive feelings. Fixated, I peered closer at the mirror, examining myself in detail. Panic rushed in as my gaze beheld my locks of hair. This was the first time I had ever noticed my tresses had become tousled. Shocked, I stood up erratically, flipping my chair to the floor. Not paying a single consideration to the unexpected crash, I raced to the waiting glass. I ran each finger of my right hand through my disordered locks, reminding them of their proper place. A wink formed in my right eye, giving my reflection an acknowledgment of approval. I was now at ease and ready for the ceremonious night to begin.

As I walked toward the foyer, I couldn't help stop to gaze into the mirror that lived on the wall next to the coat closet. While marveling at my appearance, I swore I heard an encouraging velvety voice from within the closet mutter, "Perfect." I appreciated the effort, but the comment was irrelevant since I already knew my looks were flawless. I had admired my appearance in the same mirror before visiting the Bonnets' residence; revisiting it before seeing Grace brought on a sense of nostalgia. I gave my reflection three final quick glances as I reached for the front door's brass handle. As I grabbed the lever, a sensation like that of cold stinging ice sent a brief chill down my spine, covering both arms in goosebumps. It was exhilarating and created an adrenaline rush that transported my body into a state of utter glee. It was as though a million invisible hands were tickling me, triggering me to laugh. The momentum from the laughter caused me to fling the door with such enthusiasm that it sprang open, causing it to crash against the wall. There I stood, without a second thought of retreating, face-to-face with Grace, the town's prize whore. "Grace, Grace, Grace, the town's only chase," whispered the audience member trapped in the closet. I smiled at her, but I was a fraud. She assumed my happiness was for her arrival when in all honesty I was trying to hold in the laughter created by my friend's witticism. At that moment, I was glad I had slain him, for I needed a jester in my life. The "chase" had ended just in time for Grace to meet her fate.

My smile lightened her emotions, allowing her blue eyes to slowly emerge from under the hood she wore to conceal her identity. I effortlessly read every desire her body held beneath the skin while I analyzed her soul. It was clear that riches had overtaken her mind, and the little girl had dwindled from existence. The unambiguousness of her transformation hit my vision like a ton of bricks. Her innocence had been replaced by selfish desires and flesh bound with the sinew of contempt and the bones of lust.

For a moment, I pondered her given name. "Grace" was so unusual and unfitting for such a despicable creature. In my humble opinion, which I know you all love to hear, naming her Grace was disrespectful to all God-fearing women. Summoning a person who bears a likeness to a dame of the night by a godly name brings disgrace to the word and dishonors its intent. As my eyes locked on her body, I stepped back from the doorway, allowing her to enter, thus sealing her fate. She was unaware that by penetrating the lair she had surrendered her life to a permanent residence behind the fiery gates. "Make haste before someone gazes upon your beauty and steals you away," I whispered to her as I placed my hand on her back, ushering her into the first room. Though rushed, I still allowed time to stroke her undesirable ego. Grace nodded as she hung on my every complimentary word. Her nods gained ardent depth as she took a horselike gallop into the room. Without my laying a finger on the carved wood, the door slammed behind her. Her expression mimicked the frightened look of a startled baby deer. I had trapped her, giving her no way out of her treacherous decision nor possibility of escape from her grim destiny.

The deal was so tightly locked that I swore the image of Father handing her a stamped papyrus contract and a quill for signing lingered in the now-dimwit-filled room. Although I snickered at the fact that I had ensnared her forever within these tall, unending walls, my blood boiled over at the sight of her ignorant face. Shifting my focus toward the coat closet, I noticed a flicker of light emerge from the base of the guest quarters' door. Was my sleeping friend trying to make his presence known? If so, why now? Was this his sign of approval, and was it enough for me to begin, or should I wait for Father to speak? The light flickered faster and faster. Although I appreciated the overwhelming support shown by my friend, the carriage driver, the sight inundated my body with a mixture of wrath and worry. The light was becoming brighter for only one reason, and if I were to panic, Grace too would become wary of the situation at hand.

Most people have anxiety associated with the ethereal unknown. If you saw a light flickering with no warrant, would it cause suspicion? Even I, the omnipotent, find unrest in the possibility of facing a phantom's ruthlessness. Straightaway I made a vehement decision to calm my excruciating nerves. I seized my favorite chair and struck the wood across Grace's dense skull with earth-shattering precision. The unforgiving act created a deep sound like that of a thousand bullwhips cracking in unison against concrete. I admit my rage was uncontrolled, and I was ill-prepared for the ramifications of my spontaneous action. Damn it, I was not patient enough! The bloody mess caused by my impulsiveness infuriated me. My preference would be to break every bone in my body rather than deal with the repercussions of my gruesome faux pas. As I continued to ruminate over my impetuous decision, blood trickled like small tranquil streams across my freshly mopped floor.

After further inspection, I realized the flow seemed quite pathetic for such a forceful strike. The mounting mess was so laughable that it slipped my mind until the whore's blood skimmed the toe of my polished shoe. The sight of the crimson-colored fluid made my body constrict with remorseless disgust. "Damn it, whore!" I shouted at her lifeless corpse while kicking her already-bashed temple three times. I fucking despise messes. She had to have known that! She was a pain in my ass living and remained a pain in my ass dead. After concluding my final furious kick, my legs continued to grow tense with venomous rage. My fervent shouts did not cease until my voice went dry and my body paced. I raged back and forth through the room six times. Feeling somewhat calmer, I returned to the revolting creature who lay slumbering on my once-pristine floor.

I raised my blood-smudged boot to the level of her gawking gaze, and while peering into her lifeless eyes, I executed three stomps on her face. This motion was not a spiteful assault, rather punishment for having soiled my shoes. The cow recognized what she was doing and had made a mess to provoke me. My behaviors were justified, for she was a worthless social-climbing cow, just your average whore.

My attention shifted from the unpleasant smudge on my shoe to the state of my favorite chair. I meticulously examined the beautiful upholstery for bloodstains and organic matter. After scrutinizing the fabric, I let out a great sigh of relief upon realizing no blemish tainted it. The very thought of losing my cherished chair plagued my mind. I considered how lucky I was with my taste in dark colors; the intelligent choice of fabric proved worthy of sharing in my most accomplished moments. Sneering at my mind-boggling foresight, I grabbed Grace's cape and polished the wooden legs. I then gently carried the prized furniture to the opposite side of the room and placed it in an upright position in the corner. Leaning over, I gave it an adoring kiss then left it to bask in affection from the charming shadows, for it had served a noble purpose. Lifting my gaze from the glorious throne, I turned, peering across the room to notice the mirror next to the coat closet. The majestic chair sat in silence, observing the art exhibition from afar, while the mirror remained near the evening's folderol, allowing it to capture an unadulterated image of the fruitful event. Pausing for a moment to cherish my trophy, I reflected on the deep dark isolation that accompanied the glorious accomplishment.

As I took a moment to determine the most efficient way to clean up the unwanted red excretions, an idea inundated the air. I looked toward the distorted face that rested on the wooden floor. The shape of the doorway's stained-glass condensed the moonlight to a single beam that shined on Grace's temple, creating a glimmer of beauty upon each red droplet. Her spectacular tranquility put my mind at ease with the realization that her high-pitched annoying cackle had ceased forever. Her value to a suitor had increased, as this newfound silence became her. If her family could see how my disciplinary tactics had improved her behavior, they would be so proud. "I should remember this moment!" I screeched in uncontrolled giddiness. From the parlor I grabbed a single piece of paper that sat waiting on the desk for this very occasion. Before returning to Grace's side, I checked my reflection in the parlor mirror. My appearance remained flawless. To maintain such perfection after the evening's events meant only one thing: I was the chosen one. Engrossed by the sight of my striking features, I observed with astonishment my eloquent exterior. How did my lapel remain laid, my hair quaffed after such a bludgeoning? The sight amazed the shit out of me. Never had I laid eyes on a man so remarkable until this hour.

Enough marveling over my excellence. My subservient, sleeping beauty awaited my undying attention. Wanting to please her, I tiptoed toward her in order to preserve her peaceful state. I lowered myself to the floor next to her and caressed her fleshy head and moved it toward the coagulating stream of blood. Attempting to prevent bodily fluid from staining my fingertips was challenging. I grabbed the blond locks on the back of her disfigured head and placed her lips in the pooled blood as if wetting a stamp with red ink. I then turned her face toward me and touched her crimson-stained lips to the clean sheet of papyrus. Her kiss of death was the perfect memorialization of this glorious moment; once I had attained it, I tossed her to the side. The elation created by my new memento inspired me to clean up the stagnant muck to prepare for the next day's events. To be quite candid, I wished I'd had a maid for times such as these.

I remained up later than customary that eve, cleaning until the floors shone and my shoes sparkled. You might wonder what happened to the body, so let's step back a few moments in time. As I glared at Grace, it impressed me that for the first time in her life, her horrendous nature was reflected accurately on her facade. Disfigurement and prune-blue coloring provided a perfect outward depiction of her nasty inner character. As I stood looking at her carcass, my sleeping friend came to mind. His position in the nearby closet seemed inviting, and he needed company, for I knew no one wants to be alone.

I covered Grace's cracked skull with the same cloak I used to polish the chair. The cloth emulated a makeshift tourniquet, preventing any residual secretions from oozing onto the floor. She was of small stature, making it quite effortless to pluck up her scrawny body and pitch it into the back of the closet. With the door wide open, I admired the spectacle of her body spread-eagle on top of the old man. As she had always strived to elevate her status, the match was ideal. It was quite suiting that she was perfectly positioned on the groin of an eager suitor belonging to the proper social class. As I stood analyzing my two resting companions, I discovered something was lacking. Yes, something was missing; why had I not seen this before? I consider a group of three or more a party, while just two is plain boring.

Suffering a bit of disappointment, I slammed the closet door and brushed my hands across one another three times to rid them of any residual filth. The friction sounded like muted applause, supplying much-deserved recognition for the successful completion of my quest. Filled with a new sense of accomplishment, I turned away from the guest lodgings and faced my favorite chair. A sense of approval boiled over in me from the shadow's faded edge. As I took a step closer to the dark corner, I saw the elusive outline of a devious smirk. The perpetual grin made my flesh tingle as though joyful beetles were dancing beneath it. The sensation was liberating.

Six

EMPTY TIES AND TABLES

The night was still fresh with excitement and made my eyelids flicker with anxiety. As I was pushed across the treacherous bridge to daylight with each waking hour, lack of sleep became my most prominent foe. As the sun brightened and shined through the thin shields covering my parched corneas, I knew I had no other choice than to begin a new day. Tolling church bells scratched the brick structures lining the empty streets, making my mind race. Like an orchestration cue, my bloodshot eyes opened to the ring of a second high-strung bell. To my dismay, I had forgotten today was Sunday: the one day of the week that held an implicit guarantee of morning church bells polluting the air. The notes were pure blasphemy, with a sprinkling of flattened choruses that no longer felt the need to sing in key.

Each bell sounded like tiny angelic tin-toned whispers that cut to pieces any chance of peaceful sleep. If you think my verbiage is harsh, I beckon you to think again. If you question my use of the word "cut," you might as well crawl into a grave with the deathly chimes, for I will not back down from my choice. The bells cut through the crisp air like sharpened knives yearning to stab fresh meat. Each cold breeze allowed the noise to dance through the street, carrying it to an unwelcome center stage where the nuisance weaseled its way into every pair of unsuspecting ears. The ring's attempt to cast away all the evil in the world felt defiling, the lack of innocent luster off-putting and sickening. Each iridescently toned sound acted as an ominous prelude to the arrival of my grand societal purge.

The chime-filled delusion grew to an unbearable vibration that could only tickle the ears of hounds. Suddenly it took on a new tempo, slowing in a spiteful descent. It sounded as if the human who had created the melodic sequence had become frightful of the notes to follow. If the mysterious sounds were inaudible to human ears, who could hear their music? Do you think they wrote the tune for a higher being, whether an angel or a god or the Devil? After you have determined your hypothesis, let me continue by informing the jury that I heard every obnoxious beat. I am whatever your conjecture entails; it is clear to everyone that my vibration does not resonate on the same level as that of humanity. This theory further proves my inner knowing that my actual being is godlike and requires overflowing banquets that serve only the best animal flesh for my feasting. *Chime, chime, chime* was the only sound that plagued my mind. *Chime, chime, chime* played with no end in sight. The screams sounded again and again, growing unbearable to my ears. I wondered why the melody rang so joyously. Were they aware the scum of society had sent their own infiltrators to take over their streets, rising in numbers every year? Did they know of hell's social existence in their local haven but chose to turn a blind eye to the raging disaster? These are the questions that yearn to be answered but will never receive clarity. Since the church acts as the only functioning mouth that feeds the selfish residents' needs, they, as a guiding entity, should be the first to admit the need for a purge. They are the sole perpetrators of empowering societal filth and should function as the grand marshal, leading the purifying processional.

The faithful population that maintains perfect attendance at the "deemed" holy establishment also believes in a strictly defined revelation. Like their revelation, a purge acts as a glorious way to weed out good from evil. They shall love the idea and have no reason not to comply with the notion of a tactful societal reduction. Often, I have found that those who whine about hardships are the same horrible people who have never experienced actual suffering, living boring and passive existences. Passivity and complacency are two of the most dangerous traits an organism can exhibit. Humankind loves nothing more than to control others in a quest to strengthen their own venomous ambitions. Creatures with complacent behaviors are ready-made followers for leaders with evil intent. Their laziness prevents them from deciding their own beliefs; instead, they embrace others' views, which requires less effort. Complacent sheep are the first to complain about something and the last to do anything about it. When obliged to listen to others complain, I think about using my bare hands to wring their necks until air can no longer emerge from their polluted lungs. I would love nothing more than to crush each empty head, putting an end to these fools' self-centered gripes. The feeling would be like squeezing a grape between two muscular fingers or squishing it beneath a sturdy boot. Knowing the act was complete would calm me and fill me with a great sense of satisfaction.

I heard the annoying chime again, snapping me away from my reflections. In a moment of triumph, I assumed they had ceased, but suddenly they appeared louder. The relentless ringing stopped my rambling thoughts and shifted my attention to the trepidation concealed beneath my joyous desires. As we speak, there are groups gathered inside "safe" cathedrals, feeling untouchable as they huddle in pious solitude. They listen to the self-righteously chiming bells as I battle to organize my scattered thoughts over their noisy clatter.

Maybe I should ask you for advice. What do you believe I should do with my morning? Should I remain sitting in my chair, staring at the mirror for a substantial part of my day? The activity would be effortless since my face is handsome, and I am fond of admiring my devilish gaze. Some might think the pastime would get old, but it never does. As I scanned my parlor, trying to fetch an idea, three objects captured my equal attention. The first item was the mirror, where I admired my reflection, the second a window I looked through to catch a preview of upcoming encounters, and the third a cuckoo clock I checked to ensure my timeliness to such events. I appreciated the cuckoo clock, as it only made noise when essential, unlike the bloody church bells. I always took time to cherish the bird's advice and listen with admiration to its beautiful song. While I awaited the clock's chirps, hearing the soft sequencing of calming ticks released with every movement soothed each nerve in my rigid body. The bird–infested clock did the trick, liberating a sigh of relief from my lips.

Channeling my focus on the cuckoo bird's tiny pointed beak allowed me to regain every ounce of my misplaced attention. I scanned the room one last time in the same order as before: *Mirror, window, clock.* Now I had the clarity to draft my day's schedule. *Aha! I should visit the Bonnets,* I schemed as I directed my attention toward the window. *They must long for my attractive face of conceivable wealth.* If I missed looking at my fetching reflection, they must have felt quite deprived without my company. They swooned when I graced them with my presence, so why should I destroy their hope and pick this eve to disappoint? I expect you to relish my choice of words, which illustrate my eye's view of the world.

If you missed the wordplay, then ignore my genius, but if you are following along, laugh, as appropriate, of course. Please do not agonize over thoughts of my visiting the family of the daughter I just slaughtered. Trust me when I say everything is as it should be. Since I am a widowed fiancé, it is self-explanatory that I need a replacement. Do you want me to be lonely forever? Do you believe I appreciate that my Grace is no longer awake and is now unable to meet my acquaintance each day? Just like every man on this earth, I too need companionship.

I had to offer my solemn condolences to the family and grieve like any normal love-struck suitor; only then could I move on and secure the next daughter in line. Who was the winner of my one-ticket lottery? The answer is Eve. I have yet to hear a name so delightful and simple. It rings to the highest plinth upon which love's statue can perch. "Eve, Eve, Eve, Eve, Eve, Eve," I scoffed with a gritting whisper. With the start of each *E* sound, a mocking tone chirped in from the corner of my darkened room, the shadowy voice seeming to gain power. Sensing Father's presence made an enduring toothy grin imprint on my face, the largest smirk ever laid upon my lips. It was a unique smile that was only appropriate for a particular occasion. The grin made a crackling sound as my lips drew farther apart and all at once quivered with so much intensity that my body joined in and convulsively shook. Once again, Father's energy rejuvenated my very soul. What would I do without him encasing me in a warm blanket of reassurance from the corner of my grand parlor? I dare not think of the answer, for Father is the pillar that allows me to remain grounded in thoughts and deeds.

He is my educationalist, and I am his disposable pupil. Father instructs my moral compass, guides me in the direction I must sail, and ensures that I do what is suitable for the world. His reassuring leadership will never fail me. Directing my attention away from the shadowy corner, I began my last scan across the room, ending my gaze on my treasured object, the sizable oval mirror. The beveled glass confined by the mirror's ornate frame held similarities to my guiding shadow. Neither would tell me a single falsehood. For example, if your appearance is unattractive, the mirror will provide you with an honest assessment. Unlike both of my prior mentioned companions, most creatures will tell lies, big and small, to "gain favor." Whether or not you want to hear its opinion, the mirrored glass will only spew truth.

If I could emulate any object of my choosing, I would stand six feet tall as a giant trustworthy mirror with Edwardian molding on its beveled edges. I admire the pure bluntness a mirror's reflection encapsulates. I too would enjoy having the privilege of seeing into the pupils of any organism that takes a lengthy gander. Whoever conceived describing the pupils as the soul's windows surpassed their era with brilliant accuracy. I began each of my mornings looking into the mirror just to remind myself of how fortunate I was to own such perfection. My visceral appeal is so keen that even if a blind man used sightless touch to trace my bone structure, he would recognize the exquisite nature of my appearance in the world of sight. You might think me to be nothing more than a conceded twat, but I am only relaying the mirror's unconcealed expertise. Whoever claims that beauty projects from the "belly out" sells nothing more than a crock of shit.

Once again sitting in my chair and glimpsing my breathtaking reflection, I shifted closer to the elongated mirror and steadied my admiring stare. My gaze of admiration quickly spiraled into an abyss of deception. "Damn it!" I screamed. The release of sound obliterated the room's serenity like the shattering of a marble mausoleum floor, destroying my elated mood and draining every surviving ounce of admiration from my eyes. The bricks of contempt and lurid rage filled my skull to the brim. Noticing the rapid escalation of my surging thoughts, I attempted to distract my view by using my fingers to close the lids over my protruding eyes. With my semitransparent skin-crafted shades closed, I refocused my fury toward each tiny, synchronized tick that emerged from the cuckoo clock. "Tick, tick, tick, tick, tick, tick," the clock sang, permeating the trembling air. As I soaked my being in the synchrony of the soothing rhythm, my state of mind returned to the grassy fields of serenity. "Let us start with new beginnings," I hummed to myself as a letter's worth of words ran through my enigmatic mind. The words flowed effortlessly through a meditative state, allowing me to refocus my reopened eyes. I scanned my surrounding world and methodically glanced at the mirror, then the window, then the cuckoo clock.

The ticks filled my head, growing louder with each release of tension-filled breath.

My breaths continued to calm my soul until my inner wind became so profound that my lungs had no oxygen left to take in. I had drained the room of all sustenance, and a comforting churn of dark suffocation warmed my throat. My scarf offered a sense of relief, as the tightness caused by the lump in my throat rivaled strangulation. Every breath was like my last, each heartbeat faster than that of a racing thoroughbred. The rhythmic beat radiated the most beautiful sound I had ever heard. I scanned the room again in the predictable order. Upon completing the third round, my eyes jolted to the ceiling, for I wanted a clean finish between counts. If I were to look too far left or right, the strict progression would be spoiled, forcing me to restart my day from the beginning. Before you jump to the conclusion that I possess a sickened mind, let me enlighten you on comforting patterns. Each familiar pattern creates a welcoming structure in my mind and provides consistent affirmations throughout the day at hand. When the calming sensation pierces the soul of my being, I feel the gratification of Father's presence feasting on my living flesh. Only after the feast begins am I prepared to take on whatever challenging circumstances my day shall reveal. Harboring no distractions, my day can begin with a rational mind, and this sense of clarity guarantees Father's approval of my every thought and action. Confident in knowing the utmost support was backing my every decision, I was undaunted when a sharp nudge glided my coattails to the edge of my warmed seat. As I rose from my grand chair, a surge of rebirth greeted me as I pointed myself to face the dark oak wood door, the entryway to my destiny's passage. Making my way to the beautiful sight was like a blind dance. Believe it or not, I completed the unbroken trot with my eyeballs glued shut to ease the possibility of viewing any of my three most-prized objects. We would not want to start our pattern over again, would we? My last recollection of them had to take place before my day's fortune-filled start. Like a prized racehorse, I could only pass the start line once before crossing the finish.

Before I danced my sightless ballet to the threshold of the room's exit, I threw my right hand behind my back and reached for the desk behind my chair. Feeling the contents of each drawer, I fondled a flurry of stiff papers before discovering what I was searching for. "Eureka, there you are!" I chuckled like a rooster, with sparks of childish glee. Tightening my claws around the uncovered pearl, I coiled my hand back and lifted the treasure to the front of my face. With my eyes still shut, I smelled the prize in my hand. To my excitement, the aroma of decaying iron intermingled with day-old French perfume confirmed that the hunt was over. I was indeed holding the unique piece of paper Grace had pressed against her betrothed lips. The same scrap of papyrus upon which she had laid a loving kiss of gratitude so that I could enjoy her love and affection post-death. Like a knight heading toward battle, I had received a token of luck from an enamored maiden.

Although I was unable to see the imprinted image of her beautiful red lips, I recognized their luster by moving the paper slowly through my fingers. *How lovely a day! Have you ever seen such a tremendous masterpiece?* I thought as the image of blood-soaked lips played on repeat in the cavern of my mind. Even an artist with decades of apprenticeship couldn't have duplicated a picture fueled by the amount of ethos oozing from the paper's grain. I dare say that with this piece's effortless detail and genius design, I might just be a savant of the arts. Lowering the paper from the level of my nose to my lips caused my ferocious mind's thoughts to take flight. "I want nothing more than to kiss those very lips," I squealed with the fervor of an overjoyed schoolboy as a tightened pucker overtook my face. The red lip imprints seemed so alluring I could no longer contain myself. Giving in to my desire, I dabbed my skin to their outline, the irresistible smell of decayed iron entering my nostrils. Returning the favor, she gave me a loving kiss for good luck. With an air of contentment, I refolded the paper in half. Next, I folded each corner into the crease of the fold I had just created. After my successful execution, her kiss was perfectly displayed within a single square. Holding the paper in my right hand, I gently slid her lips into my left hidden pocket behind my jacket wall, so she would remain near my heart.

As I left the comfort of my parlor, I took no chance of opening my eyes. To assure I didn't miss a single step, I walked in a straight line as though I were performing a tight rope routine across the room. I didn't look behind my exit, not even to check if the vestibule's entry was closed. When I'd reached the front entrance, I opened my eyes and, with the quickness of a cobra, seized my dashing gold walking stick and black top hat to complete my already-dapper ensemble. By now, you should know what comes next in my exit routine. Do not agonize if you have forgotten, for I shall remind you. I first stopped at the mirror by the coat closet. Can you fault me? I cannot help that I am a creature of habit. Observing my expression in the reflective glass, I assessed my image up and down. After considering my appearance flawless, I tipped my hat with a nod of approval. With my right hand, I raised my cane and aligned the gold point in my journey's direction. *Off we go!*

With my cane still raised in the air, I reached across tapped the coat closet door three times. "Goodbye, my sleeping friends," I whispered. I heard a note of morning splendor in my voice, and a slight tinge of sorrow, for I could not take them with me. Once again, I raised my cane and tapped three more times to promote further luck. Some might think I am crazy for acknowledging my sleeping companions, but I think it is impolite to leave without declaring your departure. Fortunately for my guests, I am not ill-mannered and do not give a damn what you think.

I lowered my cane to the floor and reached for the handle of the front door. My fingers touched the metal knob as I fiddled it back and forth six times. Seeing as it was now safe to exit, I opened the outlet just enough so small rays of light could filter into the hallway and illuminate the pillars. The trickle of light gradually acclimated my eyes to the bright sunny day that loomed on the other side of the exit. In a moment, the same light would rush along my face and warm my skin. Knowing the sun awaited me, I attempted to wean my pupils from the darkness to ease any state of shock. My escape continued to crack open one ray of light at a time, allowing the sun's radiant presence to be known. Unfazed by the illuminating glow, I took my first step through the doorway and let out a comical chuckle, for I knew the sun was the only optimistic character in the confines of this tale. I stand by the belief that there is never a war that ends where darkness does not prevail. I was off to the races.

Seven

CHIPPER DAY

As I walked away from my estate, many thoughts rushed through my mind, creating an exuberant spring in my step. Was this happiness? It must be what others must classify as "happiness." The fact that I would come close to experiencing this emotion at all amused me. If this was what others deemed "happy," I could see why it had a positive reputation. Warmth occupied my legs, and laughter exuded from my belly. The ravishing spirit did not stop there but rushed through my entire body. Even with this comical experience, the day did not differ from any other. Dressing in black from head to toe was my daily preference, and I believed my color choice was quite fitting for today's occasion based on societal expectations.

People often see black as having a colorless nature, while my view is quite the opposite. I believe all the shades of black reflect feelings of renewal and acceptance of new beginnings. Some find black to be only acceptable in funeral settings, which further confirms my belief that it is a congratulatory hue, even if it does nothing more than show homage to the shadow that mocks the gloomy moods of others. We should view a funeral as a time when one enters a blissful rest rather than being propelled into a miserable abyss. The moment should inspire celebration, as it represents the most peace one will experience in their life cycle, providing the sole opportunity to dwell in idyllic hibernation. Ponder for a moment this significant matter at hand. Death is not something to fear, as the individual who takes on a deep sleep state shall never need to concern themselves with a single worry. This state will supply nothing that was once of negative influence, no more opportunities for others to jab at their soul. Deep in the earth, they lie at peace, where they wait for the shadows that own the night to engulf their resting soul. From my rant, you should have gained a clear understanding of why all good comes from the color black and how it offers comfort to those living a life of hopeless misery.

As I reflected on Father's inspirations, he revealed a glimpse into the next steps of my journey. The extraordinary detail made my lungs fill with a massive gasp of warm air. With each separate inhalation of oxygen, I gathered small tastes of surrounding smells, allowing the still-standing moment to be preserved forever in my memories. The order brought a sense of calmness, for this was the moment that would lay the pavement for my future path. Once again, the image reflected what I imagined being an authentic example of contentment.

Just like the birth of a child, I would forever remember each of these days with lucid depictions for many lifetimes.

I walked toward a large shade tree in the estate's grand garden, mere feet from where I stood. My steed was secured by its reins to a majestic tree surrounded by tufts of long, lush grass and a cistern of water. Before you concern yourself over the other stallion, which was tied to the carriage on that infamous night, do not worry, for he is free from all obligations. On the first night of their arrival, I chose one magnificent steed to remain with me on my journey and released the other to the open countryside. With a quick unharnessing and a slap of his muscular ass, he galloped away, free to roam at last. The stallion that remained did not want to leave my side. At that instant, the stallion dedicated his life to me and me to him. As I untied him from the tree, I paused for a moment to regard his eyes, captivated by the entombed inferno held within their blackened cores. I grabbed a fistful of his flowing mane and hoisted myself into the saddle, now ready to begin my scenic ride to the Bonnets' residence. As the noble steed galloped, a noticeable difference became clear between this journey and others we had shared before. His gait was rough, not the gliding ride to which I had grown accustomed. The bumps in the road made me wonder why today, out of all days, the horse's gait did not exude the same joy I always appreciated. My glee was now replaced with confusion as I wondered if he too might benefit from

Father's enveloping presence. If only I could share my shadowy figure with the rest of the miserable world, roses would fall at my feet, and all would worship the ground where I placed each step. The horse's clops grew louder as his pace increased. I made out the shape of familiar trees in the distance as we drew nearer to the Bonnets' estate. The long private drive to the lacking home did not disappoint. I inhaled a profound breath of pure bliss as my eyes spotted the property closing in. I accumulated the aroma that solely filled my thirsting nostrils from the floating lies saturating the air. Disdain fueled my body as I continued my ride down the path to my destiny. "Yes, yes, now there is a purpose, a true purpose for you," I whispered as I leaned forward and stroked the horse's neck. The motion of my hand soothed him and signaled the favorable wind to kiss my cheek. The calming breeze continued to caress my bare skin, informally confirming our agreement regarding the task at hand. A gentle gust caught my undivided attention as it picked up vigor, sending a force through a branch on a nearby tree. The wind's gift of beautiful sounds created by the discreet whispers of dancing leaves appeared to be meant for my exclusive pleasure. The resonance was so obscure that only one with keen ears would hear the airy response. Luring sounds allowed the wind to guide my line of sight toward its preferred direction. Looking in more detail at the rustling branch, I witnessed Father staring back as his darkness filled the voids between the branch's wood and leaves. The sturdy bough undulated back and forth in a fluid motion like the methodical swaying dance of a hanging victim. The vivid image reminded me of the calming noise created by a clock's pendulum, counting the hours of deception. It was peaceful.

The vivid imagery of the scene, which was now cemented in my skull, caused a darkened grimace to take over my face. With great ease, the visual of a man heroically hanging from a branch became clear, his face portraying a similar appeal to my own. The striking resemblance made me imagine the look of shock that would take hold of the swinger's visage as the noose tightened around his bare neck. The first few seconds of the image played in my mind, beginning a magnificent performance. "Shh, quiet down," I shushed my mind as I waited with immense anticipation for the show to begin. I always enjoyed a grand performance, and the opening act was soon to start. The show began, and to my astonishing surprise, the main character was me! *Oh, what a play this will be!* I proudly thought. *Oh, what a play this will be!* One often goes to the theater to experience a transformative moment, so what is a production without a dramatic turning point? This matters the most, since I am, in fact, the main character; there will be no need for an outlandish plot twist, for I am enough. At this moment, I was enjoying the image of being hung like a light on a tree. The show ceased playing in my mind and transitioned to the permanency of an inescapable awareness buried deep in my core. Though I found the performance to be vastly entertaining, it also proved to be quite erotic. A reenactment would indeed cause heads to turn, and I wanted to hang, for it was my excellent idea. Though the general image was impressive, I realized a few necessary adjustments would have to be made before the next performance.

Let me continue by being transparent regarding the specific items I would change within the painted storyline. I would begin the opening act sitting on the third tree branch from the tree's top, with a sturdy rope tied around my neck for dramatic effect. My peaceful tree perching while I spewed clever puns and insightful philosophies would continue up to and following intermission. The unsuspecting audience, believing that I had forgotten the noose's intent, would gawp in shock when the ending scene showcased my masterful dive into an awe-inspiring descent from my tree. I would resemble a crow learning to fly, letting my body take flight. From the third tree branch, I would soar as if performing a Renoir-worthy art piece. Every move would be so eloquent that those observing my actions would applaud my grace. The very thought filled my body with a warm rush of energy and jitters of excitement so grand that I almost fell off my noble steed. Once I finished the spectacular dive, the rope would lose all slack, breaking my fall. My neck's grotesque snap would echo throughout the theater as my body squirmed with life's dying dance. My twitching feet would attempt a tap performance but find it impossible because of their inability to connect with the ground. Every ounce of my body would sway as I was hoisted to the floating shadows above, where I would continue to dangle, lingering for an encore. With each sway, I'd bumped the tree, creating the sound of a bass drum playing on the tree's lifeline to the ground. The thought of the spectacle filled my soul with tranquility and strength, the powerful scene casting me into a wondrous daze.

A deep shiver rolled through my spine as my steed came to a hasty stop, causing me to reenter my present being. Having returned to my actual reality's purpose, I patted my stallion's neck and dismounted with fixed intent. Upon reaching the ground, I glanced back at the noble tree, tipping my hat to show appreciation for the whimsical performance it had invited me to attend. I did not wish to remove my gaze from the tree. More than anything, I wanted to be engulfed by the willowy touch of the grand oak protruding from the earth. "Focus, focus, focus!" I repeated sharply. I had to snap myself away from distracting thoughts and knew the only way was to repeat those words to myself. Forced to come back to reality, I took a deep, unnerving breath and made my way to the entrance of the Bonnets' estate. Every movement prompted the wind to become ghostly quiet, showing respect and overwhelming validation for my aim and purpose. All seemed justified and right with the world. Finding myself at the entrance, I clenched my right hand into a tight ball. The strain of the fist I'd formed caused a dull aching sensation that ran through my fingers and up my arm. The ball of pale knuckles was raised to the height of my muscular shoulder, and with dominant force, they began my sequence of knocks. I was trying not to rush but wanted to make haste to avoid being interrupted a second time. The bold sound of three grand blows filled the air with ecstasy; they were indeed music to my ears. Not wasting a moment, I adjusted my lapel, straightened my hat, and began my second sequence of three knocks. Only after my preparations were complete would I be ready to receive all greetings. The remaining order complete, I re-fisted my knuckles. When I raised my fist for the third and final time, the doors flung open, catching me by surprise. *Damn it!* my mind screamed as fiery blood burned through my frame. I constrained my body to control my rage, restricting the anger from surfacing to my expression. *Damn it! Damn it!* I kept screaming in my mind. Now both fists rested by my sides, clenched tighter than before, as I visualized hues of red. Even the bulk of my hands had turned a tinge of crimson. My knuckle tips remained stark white, however, from the pressure of my clenched fists. The gaping hole left me standing toe to toe with the individual that had once again disrupted my structured solitude. The creature who stood in the doorway was the same shriveled woman with withered facial features who had destroyed my last visit's grand arrival. Standing face-to-face with her, I glared into her soul through the small open slits under her droopy lids. Her identity was what I had expected--a demon whore of a maid--and this was now the second time she had been a nuisance to my life. Why...why... *why* did the maid have to be such a twat? Her selfishness deserved a punishment such as my squashing her, a fitting method of demise for the vermin.

The fiery depths of my anger continued to overtake my body, and my jaw endured the wrath as every muscle clenched with angst. "Good afternoon," a scratchy, meek voice spouted. The thought that those should be the last words the maid would ever speak consumed me, but we all can't get what we wish for, or can we? I desired to wield my cane and, with all the force in my muscle and bone, drive it through the side of her skull. I craved to see the light in her eyes dim with a last flicker of diminished hope, a last gasp taken, as she shriveled to the ground in a pile of her final moment's terror, which would haunt her for eternity. All at once, every inch of my body wanted to fucking kill her. Trust me when I say this anger differed from before. I did not want to stop beating her once she reached the ordinary threshold of death; rather, I would continue until she was grossly disfigured. The thought soon became so real in my veins that I found myself subconsciously clutch my walking stick and raise it to my knees. Realizing I was losing control, I slammed the tip of my cane back down. The strike boomed like a giant drum sounding, clearing the air of all confusion. To mask my uncharacteristic action, I bowed my head in her direction, hoping the presentation would conceal the many emotions blazing through my mind. Pupils are the body's openings and allow a viewer a direct line of sight into your soul. All intentions, both good and bad, are witnessed through one's eyes. For that reason, the bow created a brilliant cover to obstruct the view of my eyes and thus my intent. To exhibit perfect etiquette, I also tipped my hat. With great composure, I asked to speak with Mr. Bonnet to request permission for his youngest daughter's hand in marriage. Finishing my performance, I peered beneath the brim of my hat just in time to see her eyes sparkle with great excitement.

Why do all women get so enthusiastic about marriage? Don't they know that by saying the simple words, "I do," all freedom will be revoked from their hands, their personal ambitions crushed? *Oh, but wait...* I winced as I chuckled lightly. *What personal ambitions?* My private joke made a quick smile come across my cheeks. The only ambitions these societal cows harbor are related to attaining a preferable marriage and being crafty at sucking men's wallets dry. My reflections made it hard for me to suppress my laughter. Their existence was nothing more than a ploy. Pondering the numerous reasons for the pointlessness of their continuation in the world reminded me again of what dreadful creatures they are. They treat the gift of life with disrespect, as if it is a mere winner-takes-all game, with no regard for their action's effects on the happiness of others. I refocused my thoughts, transitioning my gaze from the maid's drab skirt to her eyes. The disturbing livestock was oblivious to her impending slaughtering day. Her smile and nods informed me she would fetch Mr. Bonnet. I shifted my patience to wait in the entry, expecting the sorrowful news of the youngest daughter's disappearance, which, of course, I already knew about.

This was the sensational part I had been waiting for. I was dying to see the reaction on Mr. Bonnet's face when he learned of my wish to marry his daughter, the one who "ran away." Only I knew the true comedic narrative. The witticism of the circumstance remained fresh, for he did not know what truly had happened. As I mentioned, I am sure he assumed she had run away with another man. At that very moment, I expected he was scrambling to muster up a credible lie to ease any question regarding Grace's respectability. I heard a booming thud followed by quick shuffling sounds behind the sitting room walls. The loud sound resembled that of a tree falling in a forest, and the scrambling feet mirrored rats scurrying across hardwood floors. The room fell silent as I watched the door handle stutter several times. I noticed three fumbles and two bumps of the handle, but who was counting? A second later, the handle quieted, and the door swung open to reveal a disheveled Mr. Bonnet leaning in a drunken stupor. Please stand for the proverbial man of the hour! Through the ingress, he stumbled wearing a shirt stained with yesterday's dinner and this morning's bile. His intoxication carried a level of incoherence that ended all hope of a meaningful conversation. He had outdone himself, reeking more than usual of liquor and moldy bread. As he approached, his movements appeared more laborious and zigzagged than I had imagined they would be. His mannerisms resembled those of a baby fawn taking its first steps, and I relished every moment of the spectacle. After what seemed like hours of anticipation, he finally stood in front of me, eye to eye.

"Hello, Mr. Bonnet," I said with a put-on smile. I had not an ounce of organic sentiment in my skin, and only by my extraordinary performance was I able to portray the actions of a foolish, love-struck boy. "Foolish" is the keyword in that sentence, for anyone who is in love is empty-headed. "I am honored and delighted to ask permission for your youngest daughter's hand in marriage. I promise to think very well of her and provide her a life of great wealth," I said, stating verbatim every word I'd rehearsed for this mocking proposal. I continued by adding enticing facts regarding my affluence that I knew would create an irresistible proposal. Of course, continuing my portrayal of a traditional suitor, I had to address how Grace would be the best thing ever to happen to me. Blah, blah, and blah.

As I disgorged every falsehood that came across my lips, his expression transitioned from elation to anguish as he realized the disclosure of his predicament would be necessary. Mr. Bonnet knew the words would pull the rug of affluence out from under his feet. His thoughts were not focused on where his daughter might be, rather on how her actions had screwed him out of significant monetary gain and social elevation. Already expecting his response, I seized the role of the "greatest method actor to take the stage" as I channeled a noteworthy performance of melancholy. Though I had never experienced the emotion before, I had studied it enough times on the streets to gather how one should depict grieving. After waiting for a pause in my proposal, Mr. Bonnet explained that he believed Grace had run away with another suitor. To show his disapproval of their actions, he compared the devious man to someone clownish and suspected he had met her in town. I was internally consumed with laughter, for I knew he was pulling this story out of thin air. He explained they had found a letter in the courtyard the night she had vanished and how the admirer must have delivered it in passing when Grace had traveled unattended to the town square two days prior. He looked perplexed when he revealed no one had signed the letter or stamped it with a seal.

I stared at him dumbfounded, with a thousand years of grief welling in my eyes. I must have been convincing because I saw him reach for a wrinkled handkerchief he had wadded and crammed into the pocket of his rumpled coat. Seeing that he now lived in my proverbial back pocket, I seized my next move. "This will bring great shame to both your family and me since all know I wished to take Grace's hand in marriage," I stated while transforming my fake tears of sorrow to those of frustration.

I do not know why he opened his floodgate of feelings to me. It was off-putting, but I suppose some people do that when desperation strikes in these situations. "Please, please forgive her reckless behavior," he slurred.

The wheels turned faster in my skull, and sparks flew wild with blossoming ideas. With great ease, I redirected the conversational plea, placing me back to my rightful position as the hero of the story. "I believe I can offer a solution to your precarious situation," I stated with a comforting undertone. Mr. Bonnet's eyes drifted up from his feet with deepening optimism. "As an altruistic person, I am amenable to compromising in order to save your family's reputation and restore your remaining daughters' opportunities for betrothal. To mitigate the chance of rumors being circulated, I will offer your middle daughter my hand in marriage. As I am of elevated status, my change of heart will go unquestioned," I said reassuringly.

The words sounded so believable that Mr. Bonnet looked like a young child listening to a storyteller. Through my idyllic words, comforting ideas filled his mind. "You, you would do that?" he stammered as I nodded in compliance.

This plan was a winning solution for both of us-- so perfect that it was as if he were offering me an apple-stuffed suckling pig on a magnificent silver platter. How incredibly convenient. I would waste no time on coercing or hunting. The father and keeper would deliver Eve to me. "Please fetch your middle daughter, and I will provide her a prosperous and fulfilling future," I assured him.

From his slumped state, Mr. Bonnet sprang to his feet like a loaded spring; I had never seen him move so quickly. His newfound vigor was quite comical because of its substantial deviation from my prior observations of his behavior. One sizable stumble made him give up on his mission-filled march; instead, he bellowed for Eve to come to his beached location. Skipping around the corner of the hallway, she carried herself with all the composure she could muster. After spotting my face, her eyes ignited with the blaze of the brightest of candles as she rushed toward us from her eavesdropping hidey-hole. Her eyes emanated subliminal messages that clutched schemes of entitlement. She knew her usefulness was as the second greatest whore in the household. To be candid, I found heightened pleasure in knowing I was the only soul on earth privy to her much-anticipated fate. She visualized copious prosperity as she gawped at me, while I perceived darkened shadows and wafts of death. Ironically, we were both smiling at the exact moment, but for far different reasons.

"It would honor me to take your hand in marriage if you would be so kind as to accept," I stated as I extended my hand while looking into her eyes.

"Yes, thank you! I am quite content to accept your proposal," she said, not trying to mask her zealous tone. I compare the situation to setting a mousetrap without the risk of a random snap--it was effortless.

"Perfect. I will have a custom wedding dress made for you from the finest silks, hemmed for your delicate frame," I said with a gentle tone and captivating grin.

Though we had only spoken for seconds, I knew her better than she knew herself. Like all other prized cattle, she was parading as if at the top of her show class, ensuring to all that the appraisal of her worth was clear. Marrying an affluent man was all that mattered; she believed she deserved every monetary object garnered from his labors without her lifting a single finger. She had wasted her entire prudish life sitting on her ass, developing not one speck of independence. Now pleased that she was nearing the fulfillment of her life's purpose, she curtsied toward me with thanks. Do not be mistaken about her actions; this was not an actual show of gratitude, rather an act to satisfy social expectations. Before she made another peep, Mr. Bonnet shoved her out of the room and insisted on reviewing the details of the new engagement. Knowing I had complete command of the situation, I spouted sophisticated specifics I had amassed for just such an occasion, including that the dressmaker would have Eve's gown at my estate by tomorrow afternoon, but she was uncertain of the specific time because of the exquisite tatting needed. I persuaded him that a detailed timeline for the wedding was necessary because I had to leave town for a pressing business matter. Desiring that my new wife travel by my side, I said it was imperative that the wedding occur by week's end. To aid in building myself a bit of scheduling flexibility, I said I respected his time and did not want to waste it by having him sit by, awaiting the completion of the fitting, and would send word tomorrow when all was prepared to properly welcome his entire household to my estate for a dress fitting and subsequent celebratory feast.

Nudging him with my elbow and chuckling, I informed him that while the females met with the dressmaker, we would drink fine liquor together and rejoin the women after the dress fitting for an extravagant dinner party. Mr. Bonnet's listening ceased after he heard the word "drink," though he continued to nod with approval and willingness as if he were present in the conversation. After sorting the last details of the arrangement, I noticed the loathsome leather-faced maid I abhorred lurking in the back of the room. Mr. Bonnet summoned her over to escort his soon-to-be son-in-law to the egress. My presumed consumption by wedding details allowed me a plausible excuse for the intentional oversight of acknowledging the disgusting hag's presence. If addressing her were required, both our fates would have suffered. Mr. Bonnet stood in such good spirits that as I was exiting, he trailed behind, following me out the door to shake my hand. Ironically it was the same hand that had bludgeoned the life out of his youngest daughter, Grace. I smirked with my knowledge, for I knew so much, and he knew so little. *Like the adage 'out of sight, out of mind,' Grace never existed,* I thought as I took one last view of the Bonnet circus. I had to make haste to my parlor to plan for tomorrow's elaborate feast! Only the finest for my new fiancé and her insatiable family.

Eight

DINNER FOR A KING

Galloping back to my estate, I ruminated on the sizable undertaking and mused at the magnitude of my commitment. My head swirled with promises of a magnificent feast, fine wine, ample liquor, delectable food, boisterous conversation, and do not forget the pièce de résistance: the exquisite dress. The innumerable guarantees offered countless hours of hilarity for my exclusive enjoyment. Let me be clear, I have never cooked a day in my life, nor are these hands tailored to do so. Cooking causes unsightly calluses on one's hands, a characteristic found only in the lowest of classes. I'd rather perish than allow my handshake to cause others to doubt my status. Do not mock me; remember that I once lived on the merciless streets, not in the opulence of a private boarding school. The past is the past, however, and the present is all that matters.

There is an element of tomorrow's event that will quite effortlessly make Mr. Bonnet content. No matter the dinner's presentation, his happiness will be guaranteed if a full drink remains in his hand.

Lucky for me, this part of the plan will take little effort since often, before bed, I have a nightcap to encourage sleep. Believe me when I state I have liquor aplenty, enough to quench the thirst of one hundred Mr. Bonnets. Shit, an inspiration just graced my magnificent skull! The alcohol shall be everyone's feast! Alcoholics are easy to feed, for they just continue their guzzling nature until forceful sleep numbs their waking thoughts. Over the course of his life, the alcoholic pig has guzzled so much liquid fire you would think he'd have drowned in vomit by now.

Tapping my forehead with my forefingers, I finished the thoughts that were morphing into fantasies. As they vanished from the forefront of my mind, I noticed my two feet had already dismounted from my horse and strode to the hinges of my estate's front door. "Finally, I am home," I said under my breath as a sigh of warm ease released from my chest. As though it were second nature, my routine began as usual. Upon my arrival at the grand opening, I placed the key in the lock's socket and twisted it counterclockwise three times before moving the handle back and forth thrice. Then I swung the weighty beast open. "Home sweet home," I huffed as I crossed the threshold. I was joyfully greeted by the dark-filled access, the sight so perfect my breath slipped away from my inflated lungs. No light-filled receptions were necessary, for the warmth of the shadows supplied welcoming serenity.

Elation encompassed every square inch of my body as I passed the mirror and floated past the hallway's rigid walls. At the coat closet, I came to an abrupt halt. Like a soldier called to attention by his commander, I stopped, looking at the space that concealed my sleeping friends. I knocked three times to acknowledge their presence; a true gentleman must make all guests feel appreciated. Thru the door, I continued with engaging conversation, inquiring whether they had missed my ghoulish jokes and wicked wit. With no response to my polite solicitation, I shrugged, admitting the hour was late and my friends were fast asleep. Mindful of their slumber, I signified a thoughtful good night by knocking a final three times quieter than before, then moved to my favorite chair, which waited for me behind the study's walls. My study brought a sense of consistency to my tumultuous life. Each time I entered the familiar room, a veil of comfort warmed my entire being and calmed my thoughts. As I took a seat, I leaned into my grand chair's upholstered back and moved my gaze toward my glorious appearance in the mirror. "Very stunning, very stunning indeed," I said, leaning forward and resting my elbows on the oak desk. The solid wood beneath my elbows provided complementary stability to support my thoughts. "What a beautiful creature Father has created," I whispered as I shifted my torso nearer to my reflection. The closer I propelled my body toward the mirror, the more Fathers' presence grew in the corner of my dimly lit arena. The dark ghostly silhouette shifted back to the corner's edge as if to bow in disbelief at my glorious, godlike appearance.

As you surely know by now, my radiant beauty is well-known; I cannot hide the truth from anyone, even the shadows.

Tracing my fingers inside the pocket hidden behind the left lapel of my jacket, I located my token of good luck and grasped the folded kiss. I lifted the familiar piece of parchment from my pocket's silk lining and scanned each crinkle to assure no tears had occurred during our long travel. After analyzing the irreplaceable gift Grace had given to me, I cradled it. I likened the tremendous delicacy of my actions to rocking a premature child delivered months before its expected date of arrival. In great anticipation, I had waited all day to see the blood-red lips I held so dear. Once they were visible, I lifted the delicate exquisiteness to my lips and fixed my eyes upon the artwork. After I fulfilled my appreciative gaze, I gave a single kiss back, for deep down it was what my lips had been yearning for.

To keep the sweet lips safe, I laid them to rest in the top desk drawer, which I then locked with my skeleton key. The drawer secured; my stare drifted back toward the glorious mirror. My benevolent reflection met my eyes with intent, the deep connection allowing our views to unite. An idea flashed through my skull like an unexpected explosion. "Eureka! Why prepare a dinner if no one will eat the feast?" I yelled with such great excitement that the burst of energy made me spring to my feet. It made no difference if I lay the ornate feast out before or after the guests inhaled their last drawn-out breaths. There would be no reason to cook either way, for they would not enjoy any part of the delectable cuisine. Perfect, perfect, and perfect! This could not be more perfect. The reduced amount of work would bring added enjoyment to the evening. The idea was impeccable, and not one person could ruin my euphoric high. The plot's third and only remaining loose end was my addressing the promise of the wedding dress. Its successful attainment would be the pretty bow on top of my sparkling idea.

The flawless execution of this grand heist would make Father proud. To make this golden bash work, I needed to find the most lavish wedding dress one could muster. The delicate lace and ornate needlework would be the first thing the guests would want to see after feasting their eyes on my stunning estate. Their ceaseless enchantment would further bolster the believability of the picture I was striving to paint. The foremost reasons for the family's visit revolved around viewing their daughter's tailored dress and confirming her financial security. Only the grandest of fashion would be suitable for my bride-to-be, for I knew she was dying to slip the garment onto her body.

Derailing my train of thought, I caught a glance at my gleaming eyes in the mirror. With relaxing enjoyment, I resumed the exploration of my gorgeous reflection. Entrenched in my charismatic stare, I broke my patterned gaze by squeezing out three vigorous blinks of my eyes. The comforting act swayed my vision into a trance and led me to stroke my fingers through my hair three times. My features were flawless, and emulated those of a walking piece of art. I was the only entity that deserved admiration, not these ungrateful sows! Rising from my throne, I was entranced by a halo of dark light that electrified my thoughts. I imagined standing on the peak of a snow-topped mountain and euphorically rising in the air. Spreading my large black iridescent feathered wings, I'd soar into the glorious blood-orange sun, never to return. As I continued to ride the tsunami of my high, I reached over and whipped open the drawer I thought I had locked. Typically I would be enraged that a drawer was open if I were certain I had secured it with lock and key. My exhilarated mood left no room for anger as I viewed the turn of events as a favor at the hands of Father. The informal access made my action effortless as I grabbed my good luck kiss, assuring it was folded correctly. With minute ounces of precision, I ensured each fold aligned with the predetermined, unquestionable creases. Pleased with my symmetrical folds, I place my fair maiden's lips back in the pocket of my jacket, which they now considered their silk-lined second home. Overjoyed, I glided away from the chair and let out a bright-toned squeal. The freeing sound shocked my core, for it was a sound I never had heard leave my throat until now. The momentum derived from its energy caused me to enthusiastically thrust open my parlor door. It was as though it had freed me of all past burdens, the weightlessness allowing me to sink deeper into each step. The swing of my body and my heavy steps were indeed heard by my audience living in the coat closet. I hope the noise from my traveling glee awakened them, because I would not wish them to miss the party.

The parlor entrance stood wide-open. I looked back into the chamber toward the corner. Noticing the room had been overtaken by a large dark presence, I gave a slight nod to the lightless space, for I knew the corner held my dear teacher and father. Elated over his existence, I allowed for the grandest curve of my lips, which the dark figure greatly deserved. Without even the slightest touch to the golden handle, the door shut. At the speed of a wildfire burning through dry tinder, I found myself near the front entrance. As I reflected on my feelings of sitting in my favorite room, I glimpsed the closet, redirecting my thoughts toward my long-term guests. Moving closer, I knocked on the entry three times and said a quaint goodbye to my glorious fellow, the sleeping old man. Realizing I had forgotten to address my second guest, I knew I must amend my faux pas. I tapped three more times to say a caring farewell to my sleeping mistress while visualizing her slumbering in peaceful silence, her angelic lips still possessing the faintest hint of sensuality. Her adopted fashion choice was quite becoming. The dark-red color suited her complexion perfectly as if it had been created just for her. She should thank me for helping her find more extraordinary beauty, and her gullible suitors should be quite appreciative they now had a visual warning of her foul being. Like a rotten apple, her rotting exterior was only a continuation of the state of her repugnant core. From the corner of my eye, I made out the outline of my hat and cane placed near the front entrance during my whirlwind arrival. I lunged toward them and scooped them up as I prepared for my departure. My torso centered and my feet planted in the front archway, I leaned forward to touch the entry's handle. Feeling a curious warmth emanating from it, I clutched it and wiggled the golden carved handle five times, unlatching it on the sixth turn. One step ahead of my heart, my cane led the way as I walked through the large brick pillars that held the entryway motionless. Directing my gaze below my knees, I whistled as I tried to avoid stepping on any cracks that bound the stone path together.

My lowered eyes glimpsed what appeared to be a woman's shoe. The sight caused me to jump with a slight startle. I was expecting no company and did not favor unwanted surprises. Forced to stop my merry trot in order to find out who had blocked my path, I raised my gaze from the cobblestone to encounter a pair of deceitful staring eyes, as piercing as sharpened daggers. The pupils remained fixed on my face and possessed a hostile fire I'd never previously encountered. They stabbed through my very being with the sharpness of ice picks. Based on my description, do you have a clue regarding the individual's identity? Through my experiences and study, I have analyzed the human emotional spectra and could not place her within any identifiable standards. The one aspect I identified without a doubt was her look of desire, but a desire for what? This was not just the typical form of passion but a form that compelled me to feed. As my body jolted out of its startled state, I comprehended the identity of this character. To my unwitting surprise, the beast that stood before me was my soon-to-be wife, Eve.

"Oh, what a grand gesture and immense surprise!" I said with an enormous grin as I attempted to mask my anger. My insincere smile was so vast that it developed a persona larger than life. Before I collected my composure, my tenacious fiancé removed her white gloves and tossed them at me to catch. How did this woman become so vile? She had a sense of entitlement that stunk of five-day-ripened soiled britches. I stared in utter repulsion as the gloves bounced off my chest and fell to the ground. *Who does she think she is?* The cow standing in front of me thought she had complete control of my psyche when in fact I was in absolute command of her fate. Her insolence made the blood in my veins turn from a light simmer to a steady boil as fury rushed to my eye sockets like an uncontrolled inferno. My face emulated the fiery pits of hell, and I knew that before another word left my tongue, I had to breathe. At that moment, I decided I would no longer speak her name aloud, for she had lost all privilege associated with human existence. What a damn whore of a female! I must admit my initial assessment of the sisters was a bit miscalculated, for Eve was far worse than her younger sister, spoiled past the point of rotten.

Before this encounter, I considered being charitable and fulfilling her wish of a stylish gown before putting her to rest, but now my generous sentiments had changed. She deserved nothing and would get nothing. To my exceptional luck, I was saved a boring trip to town.

As I gripped my fists tighter, the surrounding air compressed my body like a boa constrictor, squeezing the life from its victim, the natural elements swathing me to cool my temper. Not allowing me a moment to think, Eve pushed past my planted feet so forcefully that my whole body shifted. Before I could stop her, she barged through the large carved ingress of my estate and parked herself in front of the closet door or, as I like to call it, the "preeminent chitty-chatty club." Slightly shocked, I stared at her from outside through the now propped-open entry. The momentum returned to my feet, lurching me toward her. My fast approach caused her glare to intensify, at which point she mercilessly screeched, "I must see my dress immediately!" Did she not think I could hear her? "I am the first of my sisters to get married, and they will not rival me. I demand to see it now!" she shouted with an entitled tone even louder than her previous command. "If the gown is not to my liking, I will not wed!" Her voice grew more heinous with each threatening word she spat. While speaking, she spewed spit from her wicked lips onto my skin and gnashed her teeth with every grotesque pronunciation.

Hatred boiled inside my core to the point of overflow, and I could no longer contain my venom. Without question, her unpleasant attitude required an adjustment; a lesson on respect needed to be taught to this insolent woman. Before I could wipe the spit from my face, my reflexes took over. Eve's poisonous tone had triggered me to succumb to my inner volatility; I raised my cane above my brow and struck her with a force so brutal that it split her skull wide open. Responding to the blow, her body fell to the floor. The inertia from the strike caused my body to follow her fall. Her foul mouth spoke no more. On the cold ground, she resembled a pile of squalid trash one would refuse to touch. "You greedy bitch!" I roared into her left ear as I rested on all fours next to her limp body. I knew my pointed words stung her flesh, for I watched her wince as each pronunciation made a new puff of air that infiltrated her split face.

As I knelt next to her, an impetus toward kindness filled my being, and I ran my fingers through her murky blond hair. She was growing cold with unconscious thoughts. Like her sister, silence overtook her, filling the room with peace. "Something is wrong with this fucking family," I muttered beneath my breath as I cradled her heavy head. This was the one moment where I enjoyed looking at the now-sleeping bride. I lifted my other hand and flicked her nose to evaluate her reflexes, checking to see if she remained limp. When she showed no signs of reactive movement, I climbed on top of her as if mounting my steed. Unlike my champion stallion, Eve possessed no beauty worth admiring, so the action was lackluster. As I knelt over her, I rolled her body to reveal her back and unbuttoned her dress. With each undone button, the dress became more fitting of her true personality, exhibiting the greedy demon for the world to see. "Filthy whore!" I hollered at her face-down carcass. The only thing that would make our bittersweet moment more satisfying was if she could act in response to my words of hate. After finishing with the last button on her dress, I moved my fingers around her corset laces and excavating the back of her undergarment until I found the satin ribbon bow.

Fondling the ribbon, I took hold of each end of the ties and whispered in her ear that her worth was less than that of an underfed hog. It was clear that she was the epitome of everything ugly within our society. After unraveling the bow, I wrapped each of the ribbon's ends around my vascular hands and, with significant force, jerked each side tighter while rendering her torso immobile with my knees. Tighter, tighter, and tighter, I pulled until I heard the sound I was seeking: a sound resembling a deer stepping on a thin, dry branch in the forest broke the room's silence as her first rib snapped. With each additional wrench, a trio of breaking bones followed. The noise mimicked a well-rehearsed orchestra providing music to my ears, each supplementary crack offering adjustments to the music's tempo. The fracturing continued to increase in intensity and sound as I moved up each of her vertebrae. Swaying to her body's music, I turned my attention to the coat closet to see if my audience enjoyed the musical performance. In synchronicity with my actions, a warm blanket encompassed my body, and a sense of security overtook my mood. Father's warmth welcomed me as we waltzed to the music. At the height of the blanket's comforting embrace, I heard the last rib pop. "You should thank me, for you can now fit into your wedding gown, fat sow," I hissed as I leaned over and bit a piece off her ear. Checking her pulse for a last time, I grew disgusted when I discovered that though her body lay still, she had not flat lined. Jumping to my feet, I knew what had to be done. I opened the coat closet door as wide as the hinges allowed, stretched my arm toward the rack, grabbed an empty industrial hanger, and returned to her side, hanger in hand. I left the guests' room wide-open, believing the second act needed an attentive audience. I did not see the metal wire as a mere hanger but a dagger of justice. And in this story, a vile sow plays Juliet. I worked to untwist the neck of the stiff wire hanger, forming the unwound metal into a straight line. With the metal's sharp end, I guided the object into her bitten ear until blood profusely poured from the canal. This shall be a lesson for all that are unwilling to lend a sympathetic ear. Why would she need hearing if she only preferred to listen to her own voice? Chuckling at the thought, I directed my gaze toward the open closet. "Is that not right, my grand slumberous friends?" I asked the tranquil audience. Grins from the dark cave substantiated my actions, inspiring me to push the rod deeper until I hit the end of the tunnel. Eve's leg kicked one last time, and her whole body went limp. Moving her face toward mine, I saw I had extinguished the light from her greedy eyes, and the shadows now owned her soul. Assured she had taken her last breath; I removed the metal rod. After tossing the makeshift dagger back into the closet, I grabbed a hefty clump of her hair in one hand and the bottom of her foot in the other. With both grips secured, I swung her body until I had built up enough momentum to pitch her into the closet with my other guests. After three satisfying knocks, I shut the closet door, the third kill of my grand scheme now complete. It relieved me to see the mess in the body's former location was minimal. In fact, the clean-up was so trivial that I almost forgot about the closet's new guest. The mere thought of having finished my third kill here filled me with a sense of overwhelming accomplishment. I lowered myself onto the hallway floor and focused my stare on the coat closet, taking a long moment to revel in the artwork that lay on the other side. It was difficult to remove my gaze from the magical door that concealed my most exemplary audience members. My fixated serenity soon came to a tragic end when I heard a pounding on the front door. "*Damn*! Can I just get one fucking moment to revel in my talent?" I hissed to myself with morbid dismay.

I made my way to the door as the knocks became more fervent in both sound and frequency. "Such a copious amount of company visiting in one evening!" I said with a big laugh that also housed a strong sense of annoyance. "Yippee," I said with a sarcastic chuckle. "Whatever will I do? At this rate, I'll have the whole goddamn town as my live-in audience!" I checked my appearance in the foyer mirror three brief times, assuring there were no lingering signs of my prior activities on my suit. Finding myself presentable, I turned my attention to the waiting entryway knob, giving it two light twists before opening it on the third. Unlike times before, I opened the door slowly to ease any unnerving surprises.

At first glance, I recognized the withered-faced woman who stared back at me. The maid... Oh, God the maid. Her presence curdled my blood so much it nearly turned it into custard. Rather than my prior feelings of only annoyance and disgust, this encounter added a bit of excitement to the mix as I realized I had been waiting for this moment. Though tempted to slam the door in her face as she approached with an aggressive demeanor, I refrained, knowing a more critical aim lay looming. She was so hideous with her interrupting manner that even a strike to the face couldn't create a worse appearance. Not waiting for an invitation, she barged into my home and made herself comfortable. "Have you seen Miss Eve Bonnet? She was to be at your estate about an hour ago," she inquired with a curious look in her eye. The glance seemed quite peculiar, making it difficult for me to grasp its origin. It appeared she was asking a question she already knew the answer to. I had a query of my own: what was the look in her eye? I continued analyzing her expression, but even if my life depended on it, I still couldn't grasp the answer. What was that look? *Ohhh, it's the look of suspicion!* I thought proudly, for cracking the code. *She knows. She knows. She knows,* whispering voices warned from the closet. The whispers escalated, inciting hatred to overtake my body to the point that my eyes could no longer see. It was as though a smoky fog had overtaken my corneas, obstructing my vision. The words whispered from the closet encompassed me from my eyes to my ears to my mind. The torturous murmurs became unbearable as they morphed into sounds replicating the shrieks of raptors eviscerating their prey. Exasperated, my mind swirled in frustration as it drowned in the chatter.

After what seemed like a lifetime, I composed myself and looked at her face, using only the darks of my eyes to guide me. "Would you like to come in?" I asked while ignoring the fact that she was already inside my home. Not knowing how to respond, she walked toward me, her shoes tracking a trail of slimy substance from the outside world. Before she could make any move closer, I darted past her. She followed as I guided the way; it was a though everything from this point forward occurred in slow motion. Stepping aside, I let her into the room first, for it was the gentlemanly thing to do.

Sensing Father's presence made my veins tingle with orgasmic excitement and signaled the show's commencement. As the maid slowly entered the darkened chamber, both feet slipped out from under her. As her arms flailed, the back of her head fractured against the hardwood floor. To be honest, she appeared to have slipped on a red substance that might have been thicker than water.

Recognizing the substance's identity prompted my body to convulse in uncontrollable laughter. Why did she not look to see where she was stepping? It was as if she wanted to assist me with my plan. The sound of her skull cracking had broken the silence of the room, her body meeting a pool of blood that encircled her hideous face.

The ridiculous fall caused me to laugh even louder, my enthusiasm filling every inch of my enormous estate with echoing hilarity. A whore ruining my clean floors would generally enrage me, but the show was so magnificent that I was impressed that the old sow had beaten me to the punch. I straightened up my posture and walked over to the body. The maid's conceited stillness caused me to miss partaking in her demise, and I realized the only way to rationalize the messy clean-up would be to take part in the merriment. Perceiving that my body had become inhabited by the shadows, I moved my foot above her split skull and, without hesitation, ferociously stomped on it. I must admit my rage might have gotten the best of me. My emotions compelled me to transform her appearance into that of a faceless figure. "Stomp, stomp, stomp," I sang, as though it were a working tune; the melody was the loveliest to grace my ears. Again I stomped, stomped, and stomped!

The motion resembled a delicate two-step timed with music composed of a symphonic orchestra of crunching tissue, the sound of her wailing screams perfectly accompanying the orchestration. Oh, my, did I not mention that, unlike the others who fell asleep during the show's first scene, the maid stayed quite awake at least until the second act. Everyone knows a maid's job is to please her master, so compliance to my wishes was required.

After a minute or three of my pleasurable tap dances, her screams grew muddled with the distinct sound of choking as blood engulfed her vocal cords. Why did the music have to stop? It was just reaching the crescendo! She ruined the perfect moment with her selfish act. Aside from her horrible pestiferous personality, she was a complete bore. Blood and brain matter trickling across the floor provided a slight elevation to my mood as it enhanced my newfound artistic genius. My Terpsichore spattered blood on the surrounding stone, creating a magnificent piece of speckled art. It was an exceptional design, a one of a kind. "Perfecto!" I said in a witty tone. The image was nowhere near perfect, however, for it was missing something key, the signature of the esteemed artiste! My body dropped toward the floor, and I took a comfortable squatting position, resting on my heels. I chose this stance to prevent getting any added bloodstains on my fashionable trousers. I removed my pristine white gloves and formed a fist with my right hand. My pointer finger remained free of the grasp and skimmed across the largest pool of blood. I performed this action so only the tip of my impeccable finger skimmed the bodily ink. My pointer finger lifted to the sky before diving to the open ground next to my faceless friend. I painted ornate lines across the floor with talented brushstrokes, the artwork so divine that I signed the floor with an elegant moniker naming the gifted artist.

After analyzing my last stroke, I glanced up at my eyes in the lonely standing floor mirror. As I stared at my sweaty reflection, I gradually brought myself up from my crouched stance without breaking eye contact. Then I reached down to dip my dry quill. With the blood on my finger, I dabbed my palms and rubbed my hands together as if I were washing them in a basin of soapy water. Once they were covered, I raised them toward the looking glass and used the thickened blood to slick my tousled hair. Admiring my reflection, I realized red might be my new favorite color. "Damn, I look smashing!" I yelled toward the glass while presenting the most enormous, bared-tooth smile ever exhibited on my chiseled face. Funny, I favor the color on women, but it appeared even more excellent on me. Mesmerized by my image, I waltzed in front of the glass. My elated movements allowed my feet to show appreciation for the floor's red glimmer. My dance stopped, and my body shifted closer to my perfect image. Bloody trails followed each slithering step of my shoes. Standing within inches of my irreplaceable mirror, I caressed the treasured object with both of my mighty hands, longing to reach through the glass and feel myself. As I stared in awe at my reflection, the sprawled maid contaminated my view, and I realized I must clean the crimson floor. I let out an exasperated huff as I contemplated the effort this would require. Though the room needed to be tidied, I couldn't break my gaze as I stood entranced by the limp, lifeless body. The artwork was so beautiful that I longed to share it with the world, but alas, all good things must end. Besides, she was late in joining the rest of her coat closet observers. I am sure they were dying to chatter her ear off--that is, if she still had one.

Nine

CLEAN DINING

The act of cleaning up the chaos had become arduous as the minutes crept on. The reward for these actions came not from the finished shine but from the privilege of touching each drop of blood that came from the insufferable wench's unrecognizable face. Her appearance was so hideous that a mere glimpse of her scared away the rats that lived under the floorboards. I swear on every grave ever dug that a filthy rodent peeked its tiny nose through a crack in the wall and scurried away to avoid the sight of her.

Refocusing my rambling thoughts, I darted to the coat closet, where I fetched Grace's imported silk shawl. I placed it to my nose and took a deep inhalation, smelling the remnants of her essence and expensive French perfume. The shawl would work flawlessly for such an occasion. I stretched out the extensive piece of fabric and swaddled the old woman like a babe. The makeshift bandage would come in handy to prevent her bodily fluids from dripping while I transported her corpse to her new home. As I dragged her by her toes, the cloth made her loose body slide across the floor fluidly. When I finished the last pull of her deadweight, she arrived at the guest quarters. As she waited to join the other residents, I noticed a peculiar response from the once-merry trio. Though it didn't shock me in the slightest, it was disappointing to witness looks of discontentment form on the other guests' faces as they caught sight of the old witch. Knowing her personality, I already had predicted they would snub her character, but I did not expect such a fierce reaction. Upon reading the awkward tension, I put her in the farthest corner of the closet possible, away from the others. I didn't mind accommodating my friends because I felt their pain and pitied that they must breathe the same air as her.

For the first time, I had found a sense of peace with other members of society. I cherished the progress of our relationships and could not let the old hag tarnish our beautiful friendships. My courtesy did not go unnoticed, for as I closed the door, the thinning lips on my friends' faces formed warm toothy smiles of appreciation. "A joyful farewell to the ghastly hag," I sang, smirking as I glanced at the shut door one last time. We were all together, happy at last, comrades for life, except, of course, the shriveled hag. I strode forward and firmly grasped the knob, assuring three lucky turns of the handle.

Closing my eyelids, I took a deep inhalation of harmonious air. As my eyes re-opened, I found myself standing in the foyer. I allowed myself a tranquil moment to find comfort through my gaze in the entryway mirror, taking the time to admire the reflection encompassing both the excellent clean-up job and my stunning appearance. My face no longer stained with red splatter, porcelain skin and cologne smelling of quince had replaced the crimson paint. I looked and smelled delicious, so delectable in fact that if warmed to a crisp, my succulent limbs would make even the most notable chefs beg for my culinary secrets.

From this point forward no one could stand in my way. Then, without warning, I heard a low whisper. Surprised, I spun toward the voice's direction. Following the calming tone, I found that the sound was coming from the corner of my foyer. The figureless manifestation reached a shape of distinctive features and vague familiarities. As I watched the metamorphic event, I realized the forming body was that of my father, the man of the shadows. He thrust his approving grin upon me, overwhelming me with eternal happiness. I knew everything I'd accomplished up to this point reflected his will, and together we stood in familial solidarity. I always have striven to be as great as him. He is my Father, and just as every obedient son should, my sole purpose is to make him proud.

I had set plans in motion from the moment of his first appearance, and my goals would soon reach completion. The time had come to reach out to the rest of the Bonnet family to inform them of the opulent dinner invitation's final details. I stepped away from the mirror. As I moved one step closer to the front door, only one thought consumed my mind: *How would the announcement be delivered?* I could send a courier, but that seemed lackluster. A dashing suitor delivering the notice to his betrothed's family seemed absurd at first, but after several moments of deliberation, my clever mind squashed the negative sentiment. Without question, personally extending the invitation would add the right ethos for the successful implementation of my plan. In addition, seeing me in the flesh during the time frame of their loved one's disappearance would help ease suspicion and protect my reputation by providing me with an alibi. I had no interest in being branded as anything but a gentleman. Looks of suspicion and doubt were not what I sought, and I would not allow any loss of control to tarnish my impeccable reputation.

Turning away from Father's materializing figure, I extended my trembling hand toward the entry door. I pulled it back and attempted to stabilize my quaking hand by taking three quick glances in the looking glass. Beholding my face's freshness assured me I was ready for the evening's events. Not a single living soul could turn down an invitation to a dinner party hosted by a man of such perfection. I am aware of the powerful manipulation I can perform, and when it's combined with my physical supremacy, not a member of society can rebuff my appeal. In addition, my fists can bash the shit out of anyone who tries to cross me, and that knowledge alone gives me great confidence. I reached for the coat rack and slipped my duster jacket onto my stonelike body. The act was so seamless that my body felt the warmth of being immersed in flawless glory.

I grabbed my cane and top hat and again turned toward the adored mirror. As I raised the hat above my head, I stopped the motion dead in its tracks, noticing I had missed a slight red smudge at the bottom of my hairline. Admiring the imperfection, I envisioned the crimson decor as symbolic of my tenacity and my soul's hidden desires. It supplied a small memento, reminding me of Father's commitment and love. The idea manifested a grin. With the seamlessness of a magician pulling a rabbit from a hat, the charming red smudge vanished. Now that my look was picture-perfect, I could leave my sanctuary. After tipping the brim of my hat toward my reflection, I rapped on the door three times with my cane and jiggled the handle thrice. Inhaling a deep breath, I opened the entrance to the outside world.

Stepping into the light, I noticed the morning had turned to mid-afternoon. The sun now shone dimmer than it had earlier in the day but still supplied enough luminosity to produce shadows. I did not enjoy traveling to the Bonnet estate in the peak of daylight, for it was too early for me to feel comfortable. Believe me when I say nothing good happens before the sunless shadows appear. My point is correct, and you are wise to listen to my observation with heavy ears. Look at what happened to my twat of a second fiancé and the decrepit maid. They both thought that in the light's presence they were safe, but a gruesome surprise awaited their naivete. Their deaths confirm my point and prove that one should trust the darkness over the deceitful light. The light exposes the world's loathsome secrets, while the shadows hold the only pure path of protection. That is why I preferred the unblemished shadows to the light's treachery, although I have nothing to hide and not a single thing in this godforsaken world to fear.

Whenever I find myself in the light, I prefer to tip my hat down to create a mysterious escape. The shadows cast from the brim of my hat cover my eyes, allowing fear to flee my deepest soul and dark ambitions to fill the void. As I was consumed with Father's call, my mind was set afire with a blaze that would continue to burn until my blood feast thirst was quenched.

Like the night, I am filled with many inner secrets that will forever remain undiscovered. Not one person or thing, including my journal, to which I confide, is privy to the magnitude of my horror–filled nights. The secrets have crawled within my veins, giving them permanent immunity to every shriek my ears have witnessed and mind has ignored. I can admit to you I scarcely know who I am and fear that if Father vanished, I would lie crippled on the floor from lack of self–identity. I believe the only force that knows my very soul is Father, and he is the only one who knows me better than I know myself. He has molded me into an excellent package, complete with embossed wrapping paper and a golden bow. Admire the surprise when unsuspecting victims dare to open me, releasing eternal darkness. I sound perfect, don't I?

Lingering too long in my self-reflection, I shook myself free of my thoughts and turned my focus to my feet. I kept most of my body covered by shade as I elongated each stride, for I wanted to preserve my fair rich skin. My skin's soft complexion acts as a constant reminder of my loathing of the light, and I had no plans to change that. Though I have assets worthy of reflecting a seasoned glow, I wanted to preserve my skin's childish elasticity.

Performing a slow, somber walk toward the long grass, I found my noble steed where I had left him. Seeing the picturesque mount motivated me to pick up my pace. I came to his front quarters and caressed his silky face. With each loud whinny, the stallion made his pleasure known. Together we shared harsh glances through our striking corneas, for at that moment, we knew this would indeed be our last adventure; our journey together was nearing its end. After I finish clearing the filth from the town, this chapter in our story would conclude. Looking once more into his eyes, I noticed his pupils had gained size with an emotion that resembled confusion. At that moment, I wished for nothing more than the ability to peer into his core and read the thoughts encased by his inner soul. The idea provoked sadness, for deep down I knew that action would be too difficult and time-consuming to conduct. Feeling my frustration, he thrust his head to the sky, and the lock of his gaze left mine. With his abrupt gesture, I knew what I must do. My shoulders sat parallel to the horse's stiff back as I placed one foot in the stirrup's loop and leveraged my body with the speed of a shooting star, swinging my leg toward his opposite side. Every bird in the sky envied the rate at which I positioned myself on the back of the steed. Seeing their expressions above, I swiftly completed my course of action, for I did not want any to become so awed that they fell from the clouds.

Thinking of what others might say if they found out my secrets made each hair on my head stand up in quiet laughter. The population I scrutinize would never believe a shadow had taught me every noble quality I exhibit. If they were to detect the origin of my guidance, they would condemn me as insane and whisk me to the asylum in less time than the brief life span of an elderly man's heartbeat. What a grim thought if I, the righteous one, were to be charged by the corrupt population as mentally incompetent. The idea flourished throughout my thoughts, causing me to chortle at the speculation. I cannot help wonder what an institution might be like. Father provided my only insight into it, describing institutions as musk-filled purgatories escapable only by death. He told me endless days pass while the dimly lit walls engulf you with no hope of lucid company. To be honest, after hearing his tales, I do not think ill of the idea. I would be content living in dimly lit confinement, for I enjoy the solitude of darkness and thrive best amid the shadows. Unlike the actual "psychopaths" who take residence there, I am a rational being. Hell, without a doubt, every pathetic, light-thirsty resident would think me king of the lot within moments of my arrival due to my unblemished mind. All would envy my glorious crown and my ability to live with Father in the confines of the haven. The mere thought delights me, and the knowledge that we will forever stand in unison regardless of life's turmoil brings me vast contentment. Jitters jolted down my spine from the rosy vision, the raucous tickle causing my feet to shudder in their stirrups. My anxious thoughts released one last spasm that filled my limbs and left through my most distant extremities. Once the shaking sensation ceased, the horse moved forward with a fervent, unwavering stride. Our unified sway carried us like a ground-splitting earthquake wreaking havoc on the dirt-drawn path. The pounding sounds of horse hooves filled my heightened imagination, creating a background noise that played across the cobblestone streets as we blazed down on the terrain. The mighty clopping of the giant equine's hooves reminded me we were unstoppable, and our shared passion made us invincible allies. The velocity of our ride left a tornado of wind in our wake. Each violent gallop made my vertebrae rub raw against my starched shirt. I attempted to orient myself to my surroundings by fixing my gaze on the distant terrain. The speed of the ride became so hell-bent that the objects we approached appeared blurred. The only item I could decipher in the distance was a crested willow tree. I confirmed it to be the same weepy creature that occupied my dreams. The familiarity made me realize how close I was to reaching my destination.

Casting an insightful eye to the future, I focused my attention on the wilting leaves I admired. I forever imprinted the image of the willowy tree in my psyche. The mere sight of it brought a rushing lick of cold to my prickled neck. Reliving the beautiful memory of my noble hanging made my gut jump rambunctiously with excitement, triggering a transitory escape to my fantasy. I relished in the moment of my undeniable nobility as my body swung back and forth, with a cascading descent nothing short of perfect. The initial snap of my neck interrupted my heavy leap with purpose, and the impact of my landing caused my tall hat to tumble away from my head. As my corpse effortlessly swayed, the wind's long fingers combed each strand of my hair. The action mimicked a motherly comfort that nearly put me to sleep, the lovely lingering picture bringing waterfalls of warmth to my spirit. My face took on a grin that spanned cheek to cheek as my imagination added each detailed stroke to the spectacular image. Shaking my head to clear my mind of the distraction, I regained focus on the mission at hand; the notion of the pompous tree was just a frivolous diversion.

The horse's bounce drew my purpose back to the present, and with closed eyes, I refocused my reckless mind on my upcoming dinner party extravaganza. If you remembered I had never thrown a dinner party of any sort, congratulations are in order! If you did not retain that critical fact, shame on you! Only those paying attention to my story will understand why, at this moment, I was full of excitement, my energy running wild with anxious turbulence. I had an immense amount of pressure riding on my broad shoulders, knowing I could not let Father down. It was imperative to uphold my impeccable reputation as I did my part to assure the destructive aspects of society repented for their horrific behaviors. The aim of the "party" differed from most, as it had turned into a necessary gesture so intricate that any sadistic executioner would kiss my feet in reverence of my strategic brilliance. The assemblage would be so tremendous that I wouldn't dare live on if anything were to spoil my detailed plan. Like an overfilled meat platter, the party would incite gossip for lifetimes. Even after the event had transitioned to a state of never-ending silence, everyone in attendance would continue to whisper its praise through all ethereal dimensions.

The sight of the Bonnet estate encroaching upon my steed enraged me. The horse's heavy footsteps narrated my heart's rhythmic pattern with thunderous bass notes. At once, my pitch-dark stallion's trots turned into a prancing gallop that exuded his shared excitement. His hooves scraped against the cobblestone, mimicking the incessant sound of the piercing screams of dying creatures. As we closed in, the estate's landscape became more recognizable; I noticed Mr. Bonnet taking a stroll in the manicured garden. Seizing the opportunity, I forcefully kicked the steed, as I wanted him to approach Mr. Bonnet with a jaw-dropping stop. As expected, because of his day of excessive wine consumption, he reacted to my loud approach by falling over his feet. Once he hit the ground, his whole body impressively sprang back to his original stature, like a parched sponge regaining shape when tossed into a bucket of water. He looked confused as he scanned the area to identify the direction the assaulting noise had come from.

As he made a full three-sixty circular motion, he overshot my direction and corrected his path to face my noble steed. His clownish pivot resembled a jig and reminded me of a dirty monkey dancing while playing crashes on a tambourine for coins. His drunkenness showed through his leather-masked expression as nauseating fumes seeped through his yellow skin. As Mr. Bonnet now stood face-to-face with the horse, his head slowly tilted up to make eye contact with the creature. The bafflement on his face was clear, and I could tell the poor bastard was still trying to orient his coordinates and figure out how he had gotten there. His eyes presented as narrow, half-risen slits, and he stared at me, squinting with even harsher intent. Each second that passed, I waited in anticipation for his eyes to close completely.

Growing impatient with his slow pace, I knew I would have to interject, for I could not wait all day. "Mr. Bonnet!" I shouted. While addressing my future father-in-law, I dismounted from my horse and tried to make eye contact with his barely visible pupils.

Suddenly he surprised me as his eyes widened, and he recognized the figure that stood before him. "My good boy!" he exclaimed. "My soon-to-be son-in-law...how are you this fine day!" His words barely traveled through his pursed lips, even though he made a tremendous effort. I could scarcely understand the mumbles that slewed out of his putrid mouth. If only I could silence him at that very moment, I would be at peace.

As his words melted together, I loosened some anger from my burning ears to assess his every inflection. With his incoherent state displayed, it had become clear to me that he had not an inkling of the disappearance of his daughter or his useless maid. To be fair, even while sober, I would not have acknowledged their leave of absence either, for they were heinous. He was just enjoying a drunken walk in the garden.

"My beautiful fiancé went to town to fetch some new shoes and will return shortly. Please bring your lovely wife and join us at my estate at half past five for a spectacular buffet and a viewing of your sweet daughter's custom-designed gown," I said in an even slower tone than before. *Goddamn it! Look at me, Mr. Bonnet!* Trying to catch his eyes during the conversation quickly became the most frustrating task I had ever attempted. His eyes wandered more than those of a weasel eyeing treats at an expansive picnic buffet. He looked like he was in a constant dumbfounded state.

The interaction felt like a terrible game of charades. We were in round one, and Mr. Bonnet's actions made it appear as if he either smelled a pile of horseshit or had been handed a puzzle that boggled his mind. I could tell he was trying to process the information I had just given his ears. "Let me fetch my maid!" he interjected after making it clear he could not discern what I had said. He was desperate to retrieve her so someone else would do the heavy lifting of deciphering the conversation's details.

"I saw her with your daughter earlier this afternoon," I said so quickly it might seem suspicious to anyone not inebriated. My words made his bellowing useless, and at once his summoning stopped. "Oh, of course! That's right!" Mr. Bonnet said with a sense of erroneous recollection. The poor shell of a man was so drunk his thoughts continued to run together like word vomit.

My smile stretched as if drawn by the tip of a sharpened pencil, and both ends of my lips curled mischievously over the successful execution of my premeditated plan. At the sight of my happiness, Mr. Bonnet's liquored subconscious took over, causing the toe on his right foot to tap the ground excitedly. His body's response to the light tap dance was unsurprising as he slowly leaned toward his twitching appendage. After what seemed an eternity, his top-heavy body toppled to the ground, nearly landing on my polished boots. Out of obligation, I leaned forward and scooped him up from his exposed bruised knees. Once he had reached an upright position, he turned in the opposite direction and tried to mask his embarrassment by placing his hands over the rips in his britches. A daring shade of bashful red added colorful accents to his rosacea-stricken face. He wiped drips of snot from under his nose as he turned his attention back to my chin to speak. I believe he didn't look at my chin out of shyness; rather, he thought that was where my mouth lay on my chiseled face. He assured me the rest of the family would join us for dinner at the invited time and said he could not wait to see his Eve's gown. He then headed toward me in a stumble-fueled hurricane of confusion, groveling and declaring that both I and my profuse wealth had saved his family's reputation. As he finished his comments, he blundered again in my direction, but this time to pat me on the back.

Feeling his dirty fingers move up to my left shoulder, my upper body's immediate response was to shudder with disgust. Trying to refocus my negative energy, I took a deep breath during the horrible interaction and attempted to shift my mind by honing my gaze toward the large picture window that sat on the left-hand side of the estate. I tried to count the number of individual bricks laid to rest around the edge of the window to help calm and distract my raging mind. On my twenty-seventh brick, two eyes met my counting gaze. The mysterious eyes stared through the opened curtains as if they wanted me to be intrigued. Peering closer, I saw two not mysterious but magnificent eyes looking toward me. They held a sense of curiosity and a look of irreplaceable intensity. The only way eyes such as these could be possible was if Father had traded his right kidney to the Devil for the pair. The glare projected from them was as though Satan had been trapped in her beguiling gut and was emanating his power of temptation through the portals to her soul. Although I could not place the feeling that pecked deep in my intestines, I could tell she had a distinct look about her as I met her gaze.

I could not look away, for I feared I would lose her attention if our connection was severed. She made my mind run in circles with a flustered will. A thought rushed to me like a racehorse crossing a short finish line, and then I remembered her unconventional features! How could I have forgotten so soon? Eureka! I had met that same set of distant eyes the first night I had made my acquaintance with the Bonnet family. They belonged to the least-notable child, the eldest daughter, the one believed to have no chance for a life or happiness. From the day of her birth, her parents had intended a life of hell for her, with or without me in it. Little did she know her lucky day was near--she would soon leave this forsaken place.

Considering she was the last daughter alive, the name Hope was quite comical, and I couldn't help but laugh at the situational irony. As I chuckled to myself, my escalating anger was diminished, and I returned my gaze back to Mr. Bonnet just in time for his next sentence. "Dapper! Then I will see you this evening!" the words tumbled off his tongue.

I nodded and redirected my gaze to Hope. "Even your eldest daughter is welcome," I said, still facing in her direction. Following my stare, Mr. Bonnet looked back at his eldest daughter peeping through the window and nodded in confusion. His red face lightened to a calming pinkish hue, and a look of unknowing appreciation overtook his expression. As his focus remained on the window, I walked back to my horse feeling at ease, knowing my mission at the Bonnet estate was complete. I was ready to make my journey home to prepare a magnificent feast, one that would not soon be forgotten. Father would lead the way, and I would faithfully follow. With haste, I mounted my horse and rode off toward my destiny.

Ten

PREPARATION KILLED THE CAT

The return to my splendid estate hit me like a refreshing breeze of dark association. My ride had never been so easily stomached, and my path was not rocky in the least. The entire journey felt as though I were floating on a dark sea of light tides that calmly pushed me to the shore's edge. Spotting my front door, I felt a gentle whisper of solidarity fill my longing ears. The tide transporting me home felt more and more stricken with purpose, delivering me to my doorstep like a package being returned to its sender. My instinctive behavior clarified that I had no choice but to relinquish myself to please Father. For a few moments, each inhalation tasted smog drenched, every exhalation emitting hopeful ideas.

The dark tide's gentle nudge continued my momentum down the path of my predetermined destiny. Though my whole life had been drowning for this moment, I felt my security vessel sink. My heart was descending to the pit of my stomach, and there wasn't a single thing I could do about it. The beating organ was plunging at rapid speed, clearing all space for Father to occupy my carcass. With the complete reign of my vital organs, he commanded my every action, traveling through my veins with each pump of plasma, gracing every inch of my core. Father's purge of my being made room for a greater purpose: he is the protagonist of this story, not me. The thought thrilled my mind with delightful trinkets of affection and soothed my tensions with shadowy, temperate blankets. I was now prepared for a storm without fear of failure.

Father's habitation had consumed any thoughts of foreboding. I couldn't wait for the night hours to cross my path and allow my dark desires to emerge. Excitement filled my bones, and I found great contentment knowing the remaining family members would soon grace my estate with their presence, providing them with a serendipitous opportunity to partake in an exquisite experience draped in ornate gold and black trappings. The grandiose exhibition would be nothing short of astounding, as I would not be responsible for soiling my reputation by sparing expense. I had claimed all admission tickets to tonight's circus; not an empty seat remained. I had prepared a great deal of entertainment for the audience, leaving them no reason to riot from disenchantment. Death is the tender for this ticket to be awe-struck, and I would not disappoint. Entertain them I must, and mesmerize them I would, for my audience awaited this performance with great anticipation. My closet companions had grown restless and were eager to observe the grand hoopla.

Stirred, I paced six times while I lingered outside my estate.

Then, without thought, I made haste to the front entry. When I reached my destination, my heart's pent-up longing eased, and it felt as though a weight had been lifted from my shoulders. My relaxed emotional state made it impossible for me to contain my whims, for I was in my haven. As I stood next to the door, my fingers reached for the knob. My metatarsals fiddled the handle three times and, on the third, opened the impervious fortress. The momentum from the gateway's swing came as such a surprise that even I found myself startled. The heaviness of the carved timber continued to pick up momentum and sent the bullish door crashing into the adjacent wall. Its abrasive contact with the plaster sounded like a blunt-force trauma and echoed through my grand halls like rolling thunder through a lonely sky. To minimize the loud thud, I escalated the volume of my textured voice. "I'm home!" I screamed as I took several steps forward. Knowing I was finally alone in my family's presence, I delighted in the awe-inspiring enjoyment sweeping through my veins. "My sweet family whom I hold so dear," I recited as I directed my full attention to the coat closet. Although they did not have to choose this life, they willingly had chosen me, and for that, I was forever grateful. As I locked eyes on the closed closet door in a trancelike state, I realized I had won the luck of a thousand horseshoes. I never had imagined it possible to be surrounded by a family as grand as the one before me. Each of their spirits lived within me, aiding Father in holding the fibers of my being together. I had heard that family is life's greatest treasure, and for the first time, I understood and concurred. I was twice blessed as my closet family was not my only source of fortune; I also had Father. He remained the most cherished being in my life because of his sound guidance, unconditional love, and impeccable management of my eccentricities.

As I took a significant step into the wide hallway, the soles of my feet landed near the iron coat rack. With both feet solid on the wood floor, I shifted my weight toward a single big toe, creating a pivot motion with my body. The act was so fluid that I couldn't help imagining my lean structure performing the final pirouette sequence on a magnificent ballet stage. Upon my last complete turn, my heavy limbs landed toward the shadow–laden closet. As I blissfully took a gander at the door's many intricacies, an exciting stench wafted into my nasal passages, blindsiding me. The odor was one of oxidizing victory; one might compare it to the scent of water–soaked pennies. The glorious bouquet sent my sensory system into overload, creating a fiery quality like that of the interior of a hot stove.

Embraced by the beautiful, dimmed lighting, my head bowed respectfully as my right hand reached forward with offerings of adoration. "My guests!" I sang, as if announcing the arrival of a royal family. To me, they were royalty, and having them with me each hour of the day made everything seem possible.

My built-up excitement propelled my legs to lunge forward, thrusting my body into taking longer strides toward the closet door. With one final skip of my sinewy calves, I stretched my right fist toward the brocade ceiling and aimed at my mark. Meeting the comforting wood with stealthy exuberance, I knocked three times.

With my ear up to the polished cherry wood, I heard their reciprocating knocks turn into an intertwining rhythmic sequence. As each percussive beat flowed into existence, the tempo became faster in pace. As I leaned even closer, I heard my guests' feet dance in unison across the wooden floorboards and walls. My body was warmed by the sound of their merrily tapping feet. Each of the sounds complemented the other and echoed through the hall like a festive jig. After concluding the last three knocks of my usual sequence, I swore that in response my guests let out a roaring round of applause and produced grins of ovation that rivaled even the most tenacious audience's celebration. My last processional beat was met with standing acclamation. Though they craved an encore, I knew I had work to do. One might wonder how an ear attached to a sound mind can hear grins of ovation; let me take a moment to explain. By now, you should know I am an honest man who has never left you in the dark or forced you to use your own imagination's interpretation. If you close your eyes and listen closely to a human face when a smile forms, you will hear a slight click, a tiny crisp sound created by the moment each flesh-toned gum becomes unattached from stretching lips. This rousing sound is one of the few that I allow my body full permission to manifest, sending shivers migrating down my bony spine.

The noise of a smile is one of many secret cues Father shared as part of the language he created solely for me. He has communicated with me through these obscurities since early in my youth, each sound torturing my mind like screeching fledgling eagles feeding in their nest. Like nails dragged across an impervious piece of metal, I could hear Father's words and knew the exact details of my bidding. Every syllable saturated my core, creating endless emotions that purged each clog from my formerly dormant veins. While envisioning the world we would forge together, I exhaled a breath of serenity, knowing of the societal reprieve and peaceful isolation we would create. Father's companionship made every muscle in my clenched body ease. Sighing away the last exhalation of my lungs, I centered myself and took in a monstrous breath of oxygen that stung of musky, rotting flesh. Long after the inhalation was complete, the residual smell lingered at the brims of my nostrils. "Oh, my. By God, I made a new discovery. This delicious fragrance will be the next cologne added to my collection!" I whispered. The crisp odor harbored a sheltered euphoric floral note hiding a slight tinge of tainted copper. Each subtle intricacy portrayed an unexpected pheromone that elated my senses and propelled my desires. The smell's onslaught created an instantaneous enchantment; at that moment I realized I was under an irreversible spell. I am damned.

My gaze darted to a darkened corner at the end of the hallway, and my slender hips changed direction. Instantly my legs led my body toward the corner as if I were in a sleepwalker's descent into the darkness. Knowing my usual pattern, you might ask, "Why not your study?" While coordinating my thoughts with the movement of my feet, I came to a quick conclusion regarding my actions. The answer was simple: I wanted a change of scenery from my cherished chamber. If this night were to run as planned, there was no room for redundant characteristics. I had eliminated all predictability with my actions and, in return, lowered the risk of my plans exposure. The movement seemed more and more right as a summoning whisper lured me closer. As each foot stepped nearer, the rumblings grew louder, and my involuntary movements caused sharp pains in my taut hamstrings. With a last nudge, I embraced the tenseness that overtook my limbs and jolted across the long room in a dead sprint. Once the murkiness engulfed my spirit, I stopped, anchoring my momentum in a crouched position facing the wall, perched like a gargoyle lying in wait for the night's beckoning call. The squatted stance positioned my bones closer to the stone-colored floorboards, merging me with the charged shadows. From head to toe, a presence immersed my soul. Comfort set over me, causing my ghoulishly arched spine to soften its position. It was as if a warm covering had wrapped around me, thawing my ice-laden core. Viewing the corner, I could see the world's true colors and appreciate everything for what it was. Turning away from the darkened walls, I held higher regard for the picturesque sight of the small room that harbored my sleeping guests and the front entry, which supplied the crucial portal for expected company. Each guest was an audience member who would witness the turbulence of my deepest desires. The notion that they would watch tonight's festivities made my teeth clench with enthusiastic thoughts.

A full minute passed while I became lost in my itinerant reflections. Then suddenly a distant, familiar voice knocked me out of my sickening distraction. Like a shuffled deck of playing cards descending after being flung into the air, my body floated back to earth. The melodious voice attempted to soothe my furrowed brow by stroking my ego. Feeling the overflowing warmth, I turned around to face the echoing noise, pinpointing the location to the infamous corner. At first the voice sounded like abstract mumbles but quickly transitioned to coherent words. "Kill..." a mellifluous male voice uttered. "Kill..." The same voice sounded again with more prominent consonants and forceful diction. The more I opened the skin around my ears to listen, the deeper the notion dug into the depths of my mind. My once-fruitless ideas grew with the possibility of materialization. If translated to canvas, the thought would resemble a solitary man wandering across a desolate snow-filled winter scene. Each of the man's icy footsteps on the frosty cobblestones made crunching sounds that intensified with each step. The noise grew louder than his pace, becoming more resolute. It escalated to the point that it pierced my ears with sounds akin to those of shattering glass. I could no longer take the antagonism. "Kill, kill, kill, kill!" The contentious words tormented my spiraling head, and in unison, the monster within me simmered with forceful anticipation. I had been groomed my entire life for this moment, for I am now, and was born, the chosen one. Sensing my discomfort, the voice in the shadows shifted the pace of his sound to reflect my heartbeat. My metamorphosis was complete.

As I embraced the calm, my lungs invited one low-bellied meditational breath in through my mouth, restoring my mental stability. My mind was now at peace, and I was free from worry. "Those in sleep die in peace," I reminded myself as a painful gulping sensation preached all my life's accomplishments. The corner, which my mind had yet to leave, projected a sense of home into my shallow gut, making me reluctant to abandon its security. The safe space allowed my spirit to think and express all fantasies without judgment. At ease, my brain realigned with my body, I scanned the room to break down the evening's required preparation. As my pupils took flight and started attacking my imperfect appearance, I noticed my flawlessly shaped body remained cloaked in my heavy outerwear garments. Raising my hands in front of me, I cracked each knuckle and reached for my top hat, which was perched atop my head. The leather band securely under each fingertip, I grasped the stiff brim. With each long slender digit's stroke, I ran my hand from edge to edge. It sounded as though the friction from the back-and-forth movement could slice through the surrounding walls, toppling my fortresses' pillars onto my limp body and crushing my bones to the consistency of dust. Holding to the same standard as the walls that surrounded me, the brim of my hat was unyielding; both possessed the stiffness of a day old corpse.

I removed my hat from my head and lowered it to the dark hardwood floor. The object's form became obscured as it embarked on an invisible descent into the shadow's grasp. Father's secrets had darkened the ground to the point where my hat became engulfed by the void of light. Thinking of the hat being consumed by the darkness that dwelt under the foundation's dust caused a glimmer of light to hit my eye. The pristine brim protecting the hat tapped the hardwood floor as I released my light caressing grip.

Changing my focus, I stared at my ornate golden commander stick, which stood perpendicular to my perfectly shined shoes. Its reflection on the polished toe of my boot made me realize how tight of a grasp I was putting on the scepter. I had seized the cane's neck in my grip with ferocious force, as if strangling a coiled snake that was about to strike. As I reflected on the image, I released a sigh of anguish from my chest as a shade of green filled my soul. Excavating my emotional state, I found I envied the snake, for the slithering reptile is a feared predator that resides in the shadows. Like the slinking creature, I wanted to be left alone to live in the darkness and be recognized by my victims' fear. I no longer got to choose my life's decisions; I had no alternative but to follow Father's direction, for if I were to keep to myself, scum-soaked members of society would continue to walk the earth like a plague. In addition, I am sure without question that if I were to sit complacently by and not complete Father's work, he would leave me to be devoured alive by a world filled with misery-laden ghouls. The snake's image now disgusted me. I cannot hide in the shadows, waiting to strike a passerby. Father makes my life decisions, and he considers my best interests and those of humanity. He has elevated me from my pathetic state to do his most crucial bidding. Envy toward the snake no longer provided comfort, and Father refused to nourish my spirit back to a state of melancholy. I must remember the laxity of my reasoning is not relevant to my true core and harboring negative thoughts will not change my sail's direction. Though the thought of captaining my ship will always compel me, it is not for me in this lifetime.

All light disappeared as I realized the precise source of the stench that continued to waft into my nostrils was that of societal garbage, not my decomposing friends. Recognizing I had just wasted time on another ridiculous tangent piled angst on my grieving psyche and caused me to act guilty, like a child who had stolen a cookie from an off–limit jar. The excavation of my soul's anguish, which for years had lain hidden under a pile of cynical dirt, was nothing short of idiotic. "I've been in this useless stance far too long!" I yelled, tapping my forefingers against my head. Flinging my arms next to my rib cage, I gripped my napping scepter and snatched up my hat. Without warning, I jumped to my feet and away from the comfort of my low hovering position. My body leapt at the speed one might compare to the quick twitch of severed frog legs. "I must get to work!" I projected my voice toward my sleeping guests in the closet. The thought of completing my countless tasks pushed me into a state of panic. I had so much to do and little time to accomplish it.

The anxiety created by my pressing schedule turned my stomach like butter being churned. Antagonized, I rushed to the iron coat rack that stood in the foyer, for I had heard it mock my mental being. Deep down I knew the only reason the structure bullied me was because it wanted me to loosen my noose–like grip around the objects in my hands; the game the coat rack was trying to play was clear. However, I could not stand to see someone torment me while I was collecting my thoughts. This was to be a time of solitude, not judgment, and the metal object was disrespecting me. Father was the only one allowed to give me direction. As I confronted the coat rack, emotions seeped from my heart's cavity. I gave in to the cold iron's desires, giving the metal stand that for which it yearned. "Fine," I spitefully spouted. "You can take my useless articles, for that is all you are worth." The rack had the primary purpose of carrying all I did not wish to bear, and I was giving its' spindly arms a reason to exist. Ignoring my disdain, I hung each adornment that enhanced my appearance on the reprehensible stand. Trust me when I say my actions were not for the benefit of the ungrateful rack. Without a second thought, I redirected my path and found myself in front of my distinguished guests' lodging. I had to let them know tonight was the night we had played in our heads and the time we had fearlessly anticipated was near.

Before I had time to partake in the brew of my steeped thoughts, a familiar routine overtook my body. My hand had lingered in the awaiting silence long enough, I struck the door like a viper, releasing my first knock. The second knock came soon after, and the third beat followed with the consistency of a revived heart. After I finished all three assertions, my guests knew they would soon need to wake, for my monumental plan was about to commence. I was to be the crowned head of a new societal utopia, and they would be the royal court that laughed at my every joke. My first order of business was to purge every evil being that had tormented those that are pure of heart and held chaste thoughts and behaviors hostage. The "clean" perspective would be as genuine as a virgin bride wearing stark white on her day of matrimony. While I held their tear-soaked handkerchiefs, the world would bow down at my polished boots and crawl on their indebted knees.

Each water-filled spectacle would show thanks for my selfless sacrifices. As I relished in thoughts of groveling, an image formed in my mind of a bronze statue erected in the town square, showcasing my handsome features. The vision became all too real as the growing darkness in the room made me realize I wasn't the only enthusiast of this brilliant development. Together we enjoyed the thought that every eye in town would rest at the level of my scrotum while their owners idolized the portrayed memorial of my beauty.

Like the elation of a bastard child when his father gives love to him for the first time, I would revel in the moment of my fast-approaching ascent. As validation circled the air like buzzards seeking carcasses, my chest rose with pride, and my feet paraded in circles toward the glowing aura that traipsed from beneath the chit-chatty door. The revelation made every breath I took grow with dominance as I pictured societies soulless kowtowing to my perfection. With euphoric fervor, my hands rose above my heart; I would absorb each of the lost souls I had conquered. "My unenlightened creatures, you may kiss my polished feet." The words rolled off my tongue toward the deathly quiet audience. Even though they were silent, I knew they were showing expressions of excitement. Noticing my speech had faltered, I made a grand gesture with my right hand to distract my viewers from my shortcomings. My right claw swirled its attached fist up to the ceiling. The dangling limb reached a state of elevation so high that it was visible to passing bystanders. My audience waited quietly in anticipatory fear of my next move, concerned what my limb might strike as it descended back to earth. Their worry emanated from the closet, absorbed by my sponged hearing, and I felt warmed by their loyalty. All would submit to my every inclination and sit in subordination to Father in a perfect world.

He can recognize all deceitful ambitions without the use of words or forceful hands. The notion that a minuscule lie could pass by Father without detection is ridiculous at best. Reaching into my left pocket, which was hidden under my lapel, I found my unique token. The warming comfort from the cherished memento engulfed my head and served as a perfect reminder of my life's purpose. Clutching the paper, I stared eyes to lips, at the haunting kiss. After slowly unfolding the parchment's last crease, I forced my plump bottom lip onto my loveless companion's pout. As I retracted my reckless chin from the page, I detected her skin's impeccable scent and abruptly closed my eyes. Standing in imaginative darkness, I entered my mind and appreciated the intricate depth of the picture's perfection. Memories overtook me, giving my blue-tinged sexuality a new tingling rush of sensation. The delightful intensity created an excitement that ran from the tip of my toes to the top of my head, depriving my skin of oxygen and turning my large organ a hue of flushed roses. "Perfect," my whisper sang across the empty room as an orgasmic grimace formed along my lips. Contentment overtook me as I carefully refolded the piece of paper and returned the good luck charm to the spot I had reserved next to my heart. I had all the confidence necessary to execute tonight's achievements.

Down the long hallway I danced as I set my sight toward the archway that led to the dining room. My joyful legs jigged, provoking my entire body to join in, and before I knew it, I had crossed the threshold of the room. Making my way through the open door, I found myself face to face with a grand surprise that made me freeze in place with a flabbergasted glare. Just when I expected my concern surrounding the evening's preparations to win over my mind, I realized I was dreadfully wrong. Father had exceeded my every expectation. The table would have served the finest of kings, from the ornate gold-encrusted plates that lay before me to the pure silver cutlery. Each fork sat from smallest to largest, wrapped in decorative napkins held together by gold threads. The middle of the elegant table displayed a heaping pile of green and purplish-red grapes. Each piece of fruit had been picked at a perfectly ripened state and exuded a juicy aroma that would awaken even the dullest of senses. The fruit looked picturesque, with ombre shades resembling an artist's eloquently placed brushstrokes. Every plump sphere's skin was so tightly stretched that any high-pitched sound would have popped it. If the scene wasn't so prestigious in appearance, I would have plucked up one of the flesh-filled circles and taken it from the vine's safety, just to hear the fruit shriek in fear.

Holding the snatched fruit between my two dry fingers, I would apply copious pressure until it hit a breaking point, the juice trickling down my unforgiving fingers. The entrancing scene propelled my body into a euphoric state. The grand scenic display had given a breath of life to a once lonely dinner table and was nothing short of perfect.

The table's architecture matched that of the oak desk tucked away in the adjacent study. The carved wood with intricate designs would spark the debates of brilliant minds. A decorative scheme of leafy vines wound around the cherry-colored base of the table with no sign of a beginning or end. The chairs that surrounded the table were draped in the most exquisite gold-threaded fabrics. The draping cut off just high enough so the complex intertwined leafy vine detail was still visible on the chair's legs. Each chair complimented the color scheme of the cloth napkins, which my guests' necks would soon be wearing. Eight royal chairs, placed an equal distance apart, circled the magnificently set table. In the far corner stood a singular seat. In the center of the beautiful fruit arrangement was a tall single-lit candle that bore an unusually black flame. The dark flicker was what I imagined lived in a haunted night's demonic eyes, and it glimmered at the thought of surpassing all traditions. The shadows had figured out how-to live-in unison with the light and used it to lure in and shackle straining eyes. Peering past the set of silver cutlery and gold-accented stark-white porcelain, I analyzed the table's naked body. There was no tablecloth covering her beautiful wooden breasts, leaving her vulnerable to the outside world. Once again, enchanted by the candle in the center, I brought my focused gaze back to the blackened glow as it reflected onto the bottles that enclosed each alcoholic beverage. My eyes drifted then above the life-stealing flame, bringing my attention for the first time to the ornate focal piece of the room.

A golden-tipped chandelier hung down from the dominant pillars that tied the dining room walls together. The monstrous fixture had features that mirrored a tree's stout trunk, and, from the body, a plethora of eye-catching gold arms were cast away at an unsettling distance. The branches vined across the ceiling and spanned from wall to wall. Oddly the sight made my stomach churn. There was no rhyme or reason to the dazzling spectacle's structure, and I found myself smitten with its maze-like puzzle. The bedazzling piece harbored endless similarities to life's treacherous twists and turns, triggering a tornado of thoughts. Each golden spindled arm resembled a large tree branch and held blackened crystals that waterfalled like sparkling raindrops falling toward the dark candlelight. The sturdy chandelier possessed an enchantment equivalent to Medusa's hair of snakes. If you were to bask in the artwork's beauty for too long, every ounce of your soul would be devoured, and your body cast into a golden sculpture. Once they were frozen in time, each victim would join with a fascinating branch, stuck for eternity in the pitiless parallel of hell's vine-filled purgatory. I marveled at the image's beauty.

Chilling thoughts froze over the streams of blood that ran amuck through my fragile skull. As the ice crystals frolicked among my every rumination, I knew a great storm was fast approaching. Closing my eyes, I called to the shadow that clung to the walls of my mind. From Father's reaction, I knew our guests were traipsing on the grounds of my estate; in a festive flurry, I rushed away from the readied dining room and frolicked down the hallway to the entry. Reaching the end of my gallop, I turned my attention to the crowded closet of cherished friends and the mirror next to its door. As I squared off my body's angle toward the beveled glass, I purged every worry that inhabited my bones. It was as if I had baptized my mind and was now cleansed and reborn, all burdens lifted, flying free.

I allowed my heavy eyes to close for a peaceful moment; a knock sounded, the thrash of excited fists filled every inch of open-air, disrupting my meditative state. The pounding then transformed into a melodic tune. In unison with the symphonic melody, boastful sounds of fueled impatience roared like hammers tearing down a heavy brick wall. I logged the tune into the depths of my mind as both unyielding and assertive. Out of curiosity regarding the origin of the knocking, I relinquished my gaze from my splendid reflection and shifted toward the front door. I knew things were about to change; within moments, I would be deemed a societal pioneer. The time had come, and my inner animal would serve Father's will through my bloodthirsty hands. Beginning with the inaugural knock and ending with the last bedeviled shriek, the purge was on its path to completion. Wailing screams would be the only thing that would escape my deathly grasp. Looking at the door, which still stood closed, I saw my destiny. Nothing else seemed relevant.

Eleven

THE LAST SUPPER

The incessant knocks continued to resound and encircle my ears. I began my destiny's final approach as I heard my residential guests arise from their peace-filled slumbers. One by one, each awoke, opening their sleepy eyes and groggily clapping their hands. Standing six inches away from the polished door handle of the grand entrance, I felt obliged to kiss it. Headfirst, I pursed my soft lips, touched their warmth to the handle's coldness, and laid three gentle pecks on it. I did this to show gratitude and reverence for what was about to come. After the third kiss, I returned to my upright stance and replaced my once affectionately pursed lips with my spidery fingertips. Touching the handle, my fist's presence made the temperature of the metal grow to a low boil. Immediately I gave the handle two familiar shakes. On the third energetic turn, my emotions burst from the seams and I flung the door open in a manic yet unpretentious fashion. The momentum made its brittle hinges creak with sounds of pure excitement. Once the door was open, the hinges presented a persona of calmness. The grandiose opening left nothing to the imagination, for the gaping hole revealed the faces of two guests. Yes, you heard correctly: *two* guests.

As soon as I saw them, my mind became burdened by an undying flurry of storm-filled thoughts. I recounted each head that stood greeting me in my doorway. Still questioning my perception, I jumped to the assumption that I had been mistaken and counted the number of peering eyes wrong. When I realized I hadn't been inaccurate, anxious panic replaced my calm demure. I was expecting three guests, not two, and the thought of someone disregarding their commitment was unnerving. Snapping myself away from my spiraling house of cards, I reminded myself the show must go on regardless. Oblivious to my panic, their starry eyes met my appearance with wide pupils. From their faces, it was quite apparent that wealth infatuated them, and they savored all the materialistic items that lay before them. Outlandish enthusiasm exuded from their stout frames, spinning my anxiety into amusement. Both Mr. And Mrs. Bonnet proudly wore outfits that resembled the gaudiest of masquerade costumes, including atrocious feathers that matched the grotesque argyle pattern emphasizing the unfortunate statures of their bodies.

Their attire alone was cause for me to want to rid the world of them right then. I did not even wish for the walls of my estate to witness the nauseating confusion that exuded from the fabrics they thought projected prosperity. At a closer glance, I noted their limited interaction with me mimicked the capacity of a child, as shown by Mr. Bonnet's lack of attention and Mrs. Bonnet's drought of words. It was clear something had happened right before their arrival, but I was unable to place my finger on what it might be. Intrigued by the spectacle, I wanted to be privy to the gossip and was giddy at the thought of a quarrel having occurred before they stepped foot into my humble abode. Steering myself back on track, I pondered the whereabouts of the third individual, Hope, who had been too inconsiderate to join. No wonder no one liked the girl, for she was rude. Ignoring their frazzled state, I summoned them to come inside. "Where is the oldest pi--girl?" I asked before thinking how the sentence would come out of my tightened throat. Silently I laughed with amusement that I almost had called their daughter a pig, and they did not notice. Ignoring my question, Mr. Bonnet nodded and barged past my planted feet.

Following closely behind him was his oddly silent wife. After pushing past the impeccably attired host who had welcomed them, they turned to face me in unison. *What the fuck is wrong with them?* I thought while observing their repugnant actions. Upon closer inspection, I noticed their eyes wore heavy with regret. Before I could speak, they filled the stagnant air with their words to inform me that Hope had followed in the footsteps of their youngest daughter. I became angered at the thought they were about to reveal that the child had perished before I could do the great honor for them. Rage trickled down my curved spine, and my fists tightened with each breath as my body tensed in anticipation of the news. *Oh, wait...* I chuckled to myself as I remembered they were not privy to the information about their youngest child's demise. They naively still believed she had wandered away with a mysterious suitor.

Catching the sight of my curious expression, Mr. Bonnet clutched his wife's reluctant hand, which she tried to pull away. To bridge the awkward silence, he perused his incoherent thoughts to derive an acceptable explanation. "Please, before I explain the situation, do not penalize our middle child or hold the message that I am about to relay to your ears against her," he said as he sheepishly looked around to make sure Eve wasn't in sight. "We think Hope has gone mad... She ran away, only leaving a short letter behind, depicting a wild accusation about how she believed her youngest sister had been kidnapped, and she was embarking on a search to find her." The words fell from his mouth like water through opened floodgates.

This is quite an impressive development, dear readers, and I would ask that you keep the following observations between us. I must give Hope credit, for she was quite on to something. It is more than I can say about her idiotic parents, who didn't have a clue about the narrative. I knew Hope had more to offer after the completion of this town's cleansing; her lionlike prowess was clear in her perseverance to uncover a world she had grown suspicious of.

Perplexed, I ruminated on the last encounter I'd had with her. When I saw her eyes in the window earlier that day, I had no doubt her imagination had run wild with thoughts of darkness. She too appeared to have been summoned by a greater force. We were more similar than I first realized, and with that fact alone, I knew she would return. I just hoped for her sake that she didn't miss the show's finale, for it would have an encore.

I continued to nod to appear sympathetically engaged in his words, executing an award-winning portrayal of concern, which fed into his worry about the future of Eve's impending nuptials. I heard my awakened guests scooting their ears closer to the closet door to overhear the entertaining conversation. "I am so sorry for your situation, and I assure you that the information, though insightful, does not change my feelings toward your middle daughter," I said softly while darting my eyes around the room, falsely exuding concern that my fiancé might overhear. The worry lifted from Mr. Bonnet's face as I continued to speak about matrimony, further cementing my web of lies. "In fact, in the other room, as we speak, the dressmaker is fitting Eve with her spectacular wedding gown. She will soon join us for celebratory drinks in the dining room." As I delivered the convincing tale, their eyes gleamed with great excitement about their soon-to-be-gained wealth. The pupils that sat beneath their corneas held reflections of robust balance sheets without a single doubt or mistrust. In perfect unison, the audience hissed louder with every devilish joke. Their requirement to remain hidden escalated their verbal engagement to assure that their reveling would not go unnoticed. In an attempt to contain my laughter at the muffled voices' witty banter regarding the Bonnets' outlandish outfits, I redirected the conversation and offered to take their coats to show a sign of hospitality. Once the articles of clothing were in my grip, I placed them on the coat rack near mine but not close enough to touch. I would never want the cheap fabric to tarnish the value of my fashionable attire.

More comfortable in the situation, I placed my hand against each of their backs and gave them a healthy nudge toward the dining room. While they made their approach to the jubilant room, their eyes took in the extravagant artwork adorning the walls. With each new painting more exquisite than the last, I witnessed their eyes widen with thoughts of endless possibilities. We took a couple of strolling steps, gingerly making our way past the coat closet. Like clockwork, I observed Mrs. Bonnet's coy demeanor shift. "What is that ghastly stench?" she blurted with no regard for politeness. Just when I was sure someone had affectionately removed her vocal cords, I stood corrected. As each individual word spewed from her crusted lips, Mr. Bonnet reasserted his grip, cutting off the blood supply to her now stark white hand. He constricted his hand around hers with an embarrassing amount of anger. His tightening hold caused me to visualize each metatarsal breaking and the glorious pain that would ensue. The blatant squeeze made her mouth snap shut and lock. She became so quiet that was as if her lips were padlocked and the key had been tossed into a bottomless river. It was obvious that her husband had informed her in advance that if she were to open her cavernous trap, their chances of prosperity might suffer. Out of lust for money, she did her best to obey his command. Though she crassly had shared her unsolicited comment, she now pretended the question had never rolled from her lips.

Enjoying the show, I took the liberty of answering it anyway. "Oh, I am so sorry, Mrs. Bonnet. I enlisted the service of a world-renowned chef to prepare tonight's meal." With every lie, I noted her pompous thoughts of exclusivity revel in each absurdity. "Hopefully the smell isn't too rich for your petite palate," I stated, following up with a light chuckle. The words stung her opinionated core; it was clear she wanted to voice a rebuttal in the worst way. It took every ounce of her being to contain the vexed fire that boiled inside. On our way to the dining room, her exterior mood changed from harsh grimaces to expressions of dumbfounded awe. My decorations bewildered her, and her vacillating reactions intrigued me. It surprised me that Mr. Bonnet's alcohol-fueled body made it to the elegant room without breaking one piece of artwork or furniture.

Bravo! Bravo! I thought, wanting to provide an ovation to recognize his efforts. Every step took them deeper into the room, releasing a grim smile on my face that bared another inch of my teeth. *Drink, drink, drink!* I heard from the chair in the shadow-filled corner. Excellent idea! Without turning toward the chanting voice, I glimpsed a shadowy figure from the corner of my eye, and my soul filled with warmth. "Would you both care for a drink?" I asked as I pointed a finger toward the liquor bottles that lined the buffet table on the farthest side of the room. Both Bonnets remained so smitten with the sights of golden accents they had yet to take in, that they functioned as though their ears did not work. Like planned, Mr. Bonnet snapped out of his materialistic gaze and nodded agreeably at the thought of complimentary liquor. His actions did not surprise me one bit, for I knew he was unable to turn down premium Scotch. After his response, his wife subtly mimicked his actions, giving an effortless nod of approval, careful not to take valuable time from her eyes poring over the chandelier.

While finishing the Bonnets' generous pours of fine Scotch, I speculated on when we would, at last, welcome Hope's presence. The clock was ticking, and I hated to think she might miss any of tonight's festivities. Moving my glance past the open dining-room door, I read the time on the grandfather clock that stood in the hallway: 5:51 p.m. The shadow refocused my attention; I knew Hope would arrive no later than 6:33 based on Father's insight and my intuition regarding the similarities the girl and I shared. This night could still run on time with a few minor adjustments. In fact, her rude behavior could play in my favor. Upon ending my contemplating sequence, I stopped myself from pouring another drop and handed Mr. Bonnet the bottle rather than the glass. "We are family now, so drink all you wish!" I said with a tone of great acceptance. To no surprise, his drunken hand swiveled faster than a thoroughbred's gallop, and before I could extend my hand in his direction, he seized the bottle from my firm grip. After extricating the boorish behavior from my mind, I bypassed handing Mrs. Bonnet her glass of Scotch, opting to provide her a more sophisticated option. I moved toward my future mother-in-law, pouring a glass of rose-colored French champagne. She focused on the beautiful spectacle of the picturesque fizzing bubbles as I delicately handed her the refined stemmed crystal glass.

She received my offer, curtsying as she took the glass from my hand. As she clutched it, I couldn't help noticing the spectacle of Mr. Bonnet stumbling into the dining chairs. Out of his necessity to secure stability, he balanced his staggering body by grabbing the edge of the closest chair back. Once marginally steadied, he tipped the bottle and chugged several pours of expensive Scotch down his esophagus. Mid-guzzle, he used his one free hand to pull out the chair that previously had caught his stagger and plopped himself in its seat to ease the spinning room. He looked contently inebriated, for he had chosen his place setting at the dining table with no intention of moving. Shifting my gaze back to his wife, I spotted her repulsion for--and resentment toward--him. I leaped at the moment's opening and seized the perfect opportunity. "Would you like me to take you to be with your daughter upstairs as she finishes her fitting?" I sounded sincere as I offered Mrs. Bonnet an interesting way out of her vexing situation.

Cognizant that a tour would remove her from Mr. Bonnet's alcohol-saturated incoherence, she jumped at my enticing offer. I pointed my well-manicured finger in the direction I wanted her to walk, and within her first few steps, heat filled the room like a gas-fueled inferno, the intense warmth enticing my soul to exit my body. Quickly I returned to my carcass and focused all my fire-filled voracity on her. From the buffet, I grabbed the glass of Scotch I had poured for her and downed every drop, ridding the room of all signs of her presence. I then set the empty glass next to the liquor bottles and walked toward her. Like unsuspecting prey being stalked by a ravenous lion, she stood no chance of escape. Our paths soon realigned at the stairwell. As I glimpsed the nearby closet, pent-up anger flushed through my veins as I remembered Mrs. Bonnets' insults toward my guests and her condemnation of their refined aroma. Of course, for that atrocious action, she would pay. She was the first to be punished. The notion made my sleeping friends cheer.

Knowing their enemy would soon meet her fate made the choir of guests grow louder, communicating their harmonic support from behind the door's seal. They continued to narrate each step we took up the stairs with additional octaves of notes. It was as if angels had descended to earth to guide us on our journey. If I had to pinpoint a place where I felt a glimpse of the God many speak of, the closet would be my answer. At the top step of the grand stairwell, I removed the candle from a nearby wall sconce. I needed something to lead her way, not mine, for I knew where I was going, as darkness was my ally. As I pointed to the end of the hallway, she continued to walk without an ounce of apprehension. In fact, I would say her attitude exuded undeserved entitlement, proceeding as though she owned the palace I lived in. She was grossly comfortable, and I rejoiced in the opportunity to wipe every ounce of smugness from her sour face. Her bossy personality rushed back to the forefront of my mind and sat badly with me. Each thought of her abhorrent behavior tasted of fraudulent copper.

When we reached the end of the hallway, I stepped toward the last door on the left. I politely knocked six times to assure we were not intruding on the blushing bride. I followed the knocks by leaning my ear closer to confirm no rebuttal. Once it seemed safe to enter, I opened the door to expose the eerily lit room. Frenzied to see the dress in all its shining glory, Mrs. Bonnet pushed past, casting me aside like a peasant on the street. At that moment, away from her husband's control, she did not lack a single ounce of her appalling behavior. As the witch stood in the room, fury filled her fiery eyes as she concluded her daughter was nowhere to be found. Her anger was preposterous. Shouldn't I be the outraged one since she had placed her tarnished hands on my perfectly pressed tailcoat?

The anger emanating from her flaming eyes boiled my blood with excitement. From the room's dark closet, I envisioned an audience observing my every move. It was time for my most spectacular performance. Seeing her enraged made me know for sure that it was, in fact, time for her to be the next addition to the celebratory feast eaten by the shadow's gnashing bite. Fire completely overtook her eyes, causing them to exhibit an abhorrent attitude of no return. I was confident that if she were to open her mouth while embracing this expression, any forthcoming words would pollute my ears. Catching her off guard, I charged her at the precise moment she opened her mouth, knocking the wind out of her and sending her tumbling to the hardwood floor. Fortunately for her, a section of protruding ornate base molding slowed her fall. It was fortuitous that her head was large, as it stuck out just far enough to take the blow and lessen the impact of her generous body hitting the floor. She immediately became confused. Using her disorientation to my advantage, I scanned the room for any practical object to aid in my efforts. I realized the surroundings were unfamiliar after remembering I had neglected to venture into this room during my short-lived stay in my new home. Out of the corner of my eye, I glimpsed something surprising: a large tin of gardening supplies. The last owner had used this unusual space as a makeshift atrium. What impeccable luck!

The choice of the room for such a use was quite peculiar. Who would use a chamber on the top floor of a grand estate to house potted flowers? Well, whoever it was deserves thanks for their brilliant foresight. I continue to lay my trust in the shadow's lap, as he provides for my every need, and I have yet to be let down. Still sprawled on the ground, Mrs. Bonnet stared blankly at the ceiling, dazed with what looked like a concussion. I saw she had left her half-empty champagne flute by the door. After darting over to the array of garden supplies, I grabbed a bottle of strychnine kept for pest control and uncorked the top. I sprinted to the leftover champagne and sprinkled a lethal amount of the white substance into what was left of her drink. My heart skipped with excitement as I watched the mix fizz to the brim of the glass then retreat once more. With my unique concoction in hand, I rushed to her side before her bearings returned and signs of her concussion waned. Her current state made my job uncomplicated. As she regained lucidity, the right side of her face drooped, and her eyes told a story of vast confusion. That moment confirmed this would be my easiest kill yet. I extended a hand to aid her in getting up; instead, she ripped the drink from my possession and, without a sense of taste or boundary, chugged the whole thing.

As she weakly stood, dizziness set in as she attempted to orient herself and realign her flawed face. Knowing the poison would soon make it impossible for her to descend the stairs on her own, I shoved her out the exit and back toward the staircase. With only mere moments to execute my plan, I had to act with a sense of urgency. Conscious of the ticking timeline, I returned the candle to its holder. Hastily I ushered Mrs. Bonnet back down the stairs to take a seat next to her husband in the dining room. Upon reaching him, she frantically tried to explain what had happened; to her dismay, however, her body would not allow her to form complete sentences; instead, she spewed gibberish from her mouth. Mr. Bonnet pretended he understood her every word and confirmed his attentiveness by waving his hand in a circular motion. The entire scene was quite comical as it continued to unfold before my eyes.

The realization that his incoherence had worsened made me scrutinize the bottle he still held in his hand; it now only contained a quarter of the Scotch he had started with. Even if his wife's babbling had been understandable, Mr. Bonnet was so inebriated that even perfect grammar would be incomprehensible in his intoxicated state. Hell, he wasn't even capable of lifting himself from his seat to take a piss, let alone help his dying wife. Proceeding with my undertaking, I ushered the crazed woman to the open seat next to her husband, and it was just in time. Immediately upon her dress hitting the seat cushion, foam spewed from her retching mouth, signaling the rise of seizures. With each convulsive flail of her body, blood joined the foam, causing a putrid pinkish waterfall to expel from her nose and mouth making her speech increasingly garbled. Ironically, in her writhing state, she had done what everyone had wished her to do: amid a violent seizure, she bit off her tongue. Uncontrollable panic read across her still-open bloodstained eyes. She attempted to open her mouth to disgorge heinous words, and as she tried to suck in one last saving gulp of air, I swear on my life that her severed muscular organ comically fell from her mouth to her lap. If I hadn't observed it in person, the fleshy addition would have gone unnoticed, forever hidden in the pattern of her gaudy gown. The most monumental part of her demise was that her own actions had caused the bulk of her suffering. I was just a cordial gentleman who had handed her a cold drink after her fall. What a clumsy woman! All I had to do was sit back and watch her ill-fated story unfold. Mr. Bonnet had made himself so inebriated that he was oblivious to the spectacle taking place next to him. The farcical sight made me release an uncontrollable laugh that matched the rhythm of the shadow's cackle. The scene I was viewing was ten times the grandiosity I had expected.

As I shifted my focus back to Mr. Bonnet, I caught him laughing. At first, I thought it funny, but the hilarity soon turned to anger when I realized he was mocking me. He had no right to revel in the amusement that was mine and mine alone. His conduct left no question he was the stemming source of the ghastly behavior of both wife and daughters. He was no better than each of his piglets and the sow that sat dying before him. He was intrusively partaking in something that wasn't his festivity, and for that, my rage grew. In the blink of an eye, I found myself face-to-face with him, towering over his grotesque slouching body and taunting his manhood. I mocked him to chug the last drops of Scotch hidden in the bottom of the thin-necked bottle. Laughter pulsing through his eyes, he obliged. Mr. Bonnet slithered his weight down in the chair and tilted his eyes toward the ceiling as he clenched the bottle between his lips. Suddenly his eyes flashed down as he glimpsed my right fist moving above my head. Wasting no time, I swung in a downward motion with the force of ten men. Rage took over every ounce of my being, and I pounded at the base of the bottle with my fist, forcing the long neck down his esophagus. With every mighty blow, I heard fracturing and rupturing sounds emanating from his throat as I forced the cavity to expand.

"Do you still find my work entertaining?!" I shouted with spit flinging into his staring eyes. Fire-filled bursts of rage shot through my once-calm exterior; my emotions no longer contained. I had hammered so ferociously that the bottle's tip breached his esophagus, and a portion the length of my pointer finger protruded through his neck. His jaw now sat unhinged, with clear signs of dislocation. Pleased with my work, I let the remaining celebratory shot pour out of his open cratered neck and onto his ghastly outfit. As the last droplets hit his lap, I yelled, "*OPA!*" for good luck. With my final forceful blow, the back end of the bottle shattered, causing tiny glass shards lodge in his face and the whites of his still-open eyes. Stepping back to appreciate the whimsical picture I had created, I knew there was no need to check for signs of life, for I had heard his final breath when he attempted to let out a last undeserving chuckle. Reveling in my accomplishment, I brushed my hands together to rid my fingers of any leftover sticky Scotch droplets and reached for the bottle of champagne that lay next to Mrs. Bonnet's vomit-covered corpse. As I downed every drop, I maintained my unbroken eye contact with her.

With the release of an uncharacteristic belch, I cringed and wiped the fizz from my lips. Spruced up, I looked toward Mr. Bonnet and saluted his still-vertical body. Tossing the empty bottle of champagne toward him, I grinned as the glass shattered at his feet. "Mr. Bonnet, would you care for another drink?" I asked while laughing as though I had just told the best joke of my life. My eyes shifted toward the grandfather clock that waited patiently outside the dining room entry. When I realized it was only 6:20 p.m., my body warmed with a sense of achievement because, just as planned, I was early for my last guest's arrival. Without a care in the world, I reviewed the spectacle; this was always the plan, and I was closer than ever to its completion. With thirteen minutes to spare, I was the king of the party and graciously invited the rest of my waiting guests to join me for dinner. Without recollection of my footsteps, I found myself enthusiastically knocking at the coat closet. Two sets of three. Being a polite gentleman, I wanted to make them aware of my presence before barging into their private lodging and extending the invitation. This would be fun. The opening motion of the creaking door made the bodies tumble toward me, accompanied by the stench of dried blood and shit. As I stared at their discolored eyes and rotting flesh, I immediately realized I didn't want to touch them, then remembered their dedication to my success. I had no choice, as they were unable to walk to the dinner table on their own. With each step, my disgust grew, and dry heaves ensued. One by one, I reluctantly dragged each guest and placed them at their rightful seat around the dining room table. When I finished the loathsome chore, every ounce of my energy was drained, and the limited stamina I had left was held by a puny thread. Sweat dripping from my furrowed brow, I lifted the last body, that of the carriage driver, into his waiting seat. Standing at the table, I analyzed each of my friends' distinct faces, taking a moment to revel in our accomplishments. With all my guests assembled for the first time, I realized the significance of my actions; Father and I were unstoppable. Hearing a slight sound, I turned in time to detect that the chair placed in the shadow's corner moved as Father took his seat and joined us. With only one body left to complete our mission, I took a long moment to speak with my father, the glorious shadow. As I conferred with his presence, I sensed the heads of my disfigured audience members turn, acknowledging the master of the show. Father responded to each word I shared by filling my ears with comforting assurances and whispering thoughts regarding my future prosperity. Each word resembled a cool breeze brushing my cheek, blowing lingering painful memories into permanent silence. He was pleased and I was content. To my dismay, the grandfather clock's chimes blasting through the hall shattered the enlightening conversation. The carved bird chirped from its wooden enclosure, letting me know it was indeed six thirty-three. The time had arrived. A knock resounded from the grand entrance in unison with each clock's chime, just as the shadow had foretold. *I love a punctual woman*, I thought, laughing as I looked toward the lone seat in the corner. If one weren't careful, he or she might have overlooked his presence by not recognizing the slight indentations on the seat cushion from his body weight, which anchored the chair to the floor. Gleefully I danced toward the foyer mirror. Knowing my appearance was presentable, I kicked the half-opened closet door closed and braced myself for the evening's grand finale.

Twelve

THE GRAND FINALE

The moment of the denouement had arrived. The most anticipated event of the night was about to take place, and to achieve the most tremendous success, I recognized I must cleanse my mind's palate by ridding my brain of any performance anxiety that might creep in and derail the night's plan. This upcoming performance was the show's highlight, and I refused to disappoint. It would be so grand that Shakespeare himself would forever roll in his grave with envy over my ingenious theatricals. Exuberance overtook each of my limbs, signaling the show was soon to begin. Welcoming the rush of glee running through my legs, I tapped my right foot three times, then my left, before I opened the door. I turned the handle slowly to show demure, alleviating any possibility of suspicious thoughts.

With the entry open, I saw a female figure standing before me, and gloriously it was the woman of the hour, Hope. She was the missing puzzle piece I craved, and for the first time, I concluded her name was befitting. She would become the pioneer of the world's greatest revelation, her demise a monumental moment read about in history books for generations to come. Hope stood before me as the chosen one, the sacrificial lamb, whose oblation would cleanse this hellhole of a town. As I stood in reverent introspection, the shadow prompted a single tear to form in my left eye. With the release of the droplet, happiness deluged my mind. Just one glance at her silhouette, and she captured me. I pinched my skin to ensure the encounter wasn't a hallucination, for I found it astonishing that I felt eerily connected to her. Although there was something different about Hope, something peculiar about her demeanor, I was unable to put my finger on the aberration that tormented my consciousness. Her eyes contemplated my tousled hair, and she shot a skeptical glance at me. Disregarding her intuition, she continued ahead on her path to enter my home. Her motion was robotic, both feet looking as though sheer obedience drove them. She had been told to meet her family here, and as a result, she had to follow their direction. As she stepped through the shadowy entry, her eyes darted around, scanning every dim crevice. I stared in fascination as her gaze abruptly fixated on a distant shadowed corner. Analyzing her expression, I watched as her eyes widened and she looked as though she recognized a familiar face. So many unanswered questions flashed through my mind, all revolving around the peculiar stare she continued to unleash. Was it possible she had discovered Father and did she receive the same love I experienced whenever his voice spoke to me? I leaned closer to study each of Hope's pointed facial features. During my analysis, I noticed a freshly bruised eye in the beginning stages of healing; the spot appeared to have served as the target of abhorrent loathing. Unable to control my infringement of her space, I advanced closer to continue my investigation and solve her perplexing enigma. Captivation consumed me to the point that I was startled by our proximity. Upon realizing my transgression, I shifted my body closer to the front door, the same massive framework that had invited her in to complete her destiny. As I stood next to the helpful ally, I heard the shadow's voice command me to seal us away from the outside world. With valiant obedience, I locked the hinged beast. Throughout the room, the click of the lock reverberated like a musical tone, the sound complimenting the shadow's low chants from the dark corner.

Closing my eyes, I focused my traversing mind and listened to the shadow's words echoing from a distance. *Swallow the key that allows her to leave,* the deep voice said, infiltrating my muddled mind. Without hesitation, I reached into my pocket, fumbling for the key that had been left to drown in its depths. At last, my fingers met the cold iron skeleton key, the one item that would allow Hope to escape from hell. With the key tightly in my hand, I waited for a moment when she appeared at her greatest point of distraction. Her eyes redirected from where I stood and shifted toward the artwork in the hallway; without a moment's hesitation, I seized the opportunity. I turned my attention from Hope and compulsively pushed the cold metal object to the back of my throat, forcefully swallowing the ornate skeleton key. As it clawed its way down my windpipe, a sigh of relief left my core, for I knew we were alone and free from all forms of disruption. Disposing of the key guaranteed that neither of us could escape our fate; I was forcing us to take the journey side by side.

Knowing we had all the time in the world to execute our night's endeavor, I transferred my attention back to her facial structure. As I studied her complexion, I found it fascinating that she didn't resemble Mr. Bonnet, as both of his other daughters had received his genetic characteristics for either the lips or nose. Unlike her putrid sisters, Hope had no similarities imprinted on her appearance. An epiphany hit my skull like a bag of bricks as I realized the likely cause of her family's brutal mistreatment. Was she a child born of a secret affair? Was that why the parents had no love for her? Just like my own, I knew they had built her life on a bed of lies and atrocious abuse. Shivers quaked across my rib cage as the fact that they had cut us from the same cloth trolled my mind.

Hope's naive hesitancy suited her malnourished frame, reinforcing the speculation that nothing about her seemed quite right. Obsessing on her situation, I realized she needed Father's help, which she would generously receive. Seeing her engrossed cerebral state, I snatched the moment to cross the room to the nearest windows in a catlike manner. Since both the shadow and I do not favor unwelcome guests, we had agreed to seal ourselves away from the outside world by applying glue-like substances to each windowsill to cement them shut. Sometimes I am so consumed by the shadow's thoughts that I can't recollect whether he or I completed a task, so I thought it best to investigate to ensure that all the windows' bonds had cured. I gave the windowsills three quick tugs and took a lasting mental image to note I had eliminated all potential routes of escape. Knowing the Shadow had my best interest in mind gave me great comfort.

With the key consumed and the impervious windows double-checked, I knew I had trapped her with no hope of avoiding this life-changing moment. While shifting my body back to my original location, I caught her gaze and spotted her eyes analyze every inch of my body. Her methodical approach toward examining her surroundings made me realize her intellect was beyond that of an average woman. She was strikingly observant and possessed a much quicker wit. As I stared deeply into her irises, I witnessed a show of hunger and a yearning for acceptance. Slowly I unwrapped the tie from my neck and approached her. As I moved closer, her instincts took over, guiding her to step in the opposite direction. "I will not hurt you," I told her as I continued my approach while maintaining an assuring tone. Her glance loosened as she listened intently to my every word. Her pupils then migrated back to fixate on the shadowy corner. I followed her redirected stare, for I wanted to know what was engaging her attention and drawing her away from my charm. Was Father letting her know everything was okay? Did she already know how her destiny would end? Shaking my head, I ignored my hurt ego; then, after clearing my throat, I continued with the plan. "You know how Eve can be endearingly eccentric. As part of her extravagant wishes, she desires that each family member wear a blindfold when entering the dining room, so she can reveal the surprise of her glorious white gown." When I heard the words leave my lips, they seemed flawed. I wasn't happy with my performance yet Hope seemed to absorb every ounce of the tale. Her trust in others, which many in society would find endearing, would be her demise. Not expecting her to enter this situation with a blind eye, I concluded she could only have such a trusting demeanor because Father had enlightened her. Although overwrought with the curiosity over whether Father had spoken to her, I knew now wasn't the time or place for the question to prompt potential conflict or confusion. Hope deserved a tranquil last moment in this world, and that was what she would get.

Calmly I approached her from behind and fettered a blindfold around her eyes, tightening it just enough to obstruct all her optics. After I knotted the two loose ends, I swept my fingers through her tousled hair, delicately pushing it behind each ear. While shifting the last strands with my left hand, I forcefully used my right to strike her neck. I landed my knuckles with enough ferocity against her pressure point that it caused her body to collapse unconsciously to the floor. Witnessing the beauty of her delicate body adorning the blindfold forced incongruous feelings to frolic across my chest, injecting breath into my dead heart.

The positioning of Hope's tranquil frame made her look as though she had just performed a beautiful cabriole. Her balletic legs appeared tired from the first half of the performance, so she rested during intermission. With my body lowered beside her, I caressed her then scooped my hands under her limp frame and effortlessly lifted her from the floor. She resembled a small child as I cradled her and rocked her body back and forth. While soothingly swaying her, I freed a hand to brush away a sole strand of hair gracing her eyes. I continued to use my other hand to support each vertebra that protruded from her coiled back. The resting peace exhibited by her limbs showed me that for the first time in her life she seemed protected and not fearful of what her day's abuse would entail.

Gripping her in my arms, I rose to my feet. With each attentive step, I transported her to the dining room to coalesce with the other guests. Before placing her at the table, I humanely identified which partygoers would appear painfully familiar, unrecognizable, and refreshingly new to her waking eyes. Once I reached the chambranle, I took an exact thirty-three seconds to glance over my left shoulder and check the time on the grandfather clock behind me. Engrossed with the ticking hands, I noted the clock read 6:51 on the dot, and with that realization, my viscera exuded feelings of equanimity. I calmed my intuitive mind, knowing the evening remained right on schedule; the unnatural serenity clarified that we were just the shadow's puppets performing in a masterful show. The tug of a string controlled our lives as we performed at his highest inclination, and he solely held power to change our lives forever. I must confess I have concealed an essential reality in my sharing of this tale and believe this is the moment to unveil the truth. From the first moment Father whispered my life's true purpose in my ear, I found my efforts to stop my wicked thoughts and actions were futile despite my desperate attempts.

We arrived through the dining room archway as one being rather than two and made our way to the ostentatious dining table. I positioned Hope's lifeless body on the second-to-last chair, so she sat straight across the table from me, knowing that when her eyes awoke, the sight of my conscious presence would calm her. In addition, Hope's designated seat stood between Mr. Bonnet, her counterfeit father, and dear Grace, my first betrothed. I concluded that this locality would suit her, considering these individuals' personalities were by far the most bearable out of all the dinner fellows. Envisioning the expression that would soon flash across her face made me howl with excitement. When at last she awakened to the sight that encompassed her and revealed the eradication of her life's pestilence, an overwhelming sense of rebirth would flood her bosom.

After placing her body at the table, I realized I must secure it for her to maintain an upright position. Posthaste, I surveyed the chamber, searching for something to anchor her legs; my eyes noted the decorations surrounding her, specifically the tapestry cords that adorned each banquet chair, which would perfectly restrain her limbs and prevent any flailing. Like someone frantically waves their arms while gasping for air during a drowning, she no doubt would attempt similar frenetic movements to free herself. As I scrutinized her body's position again, I left her blindfold on. Wanting to ease any added shock she might feel as she acclimated, I took all precautions to diminish unnecessary pandemonium; I had to execute the impending ceremony. Believe me when I say she was the last person I would allow to ruin the master plan, and I intended to do everything in my power to prevent that from happening. Once I'd secured ties around her wrists and ankles, I ran my curious fingers across each of her scarcely discernible womanly curves. Experiencing a moment of gratification, I grazed my nose up the nape of her neck to the lobe of her ear, smelling her delicate skin along the way. With the gentled stroke of my fingers, I traced the line of her jaw and brushed the hair back from her blindfolded eyes. Touching the shape of her face with my fingertips, I lightly flicked each of her high cheekbones. The comforting act brought me closer than ever to my Fatherly figure.

Each caress of Hope's porcelain skin provoked heightened excitement through my body cavity, while anticipation of the performance surged through my mind. The show was about to begin. My impatience might kill me if I had to wait any longer. In fact, my core became so restless that my lips released tiny spurts of hardened air upon the girl's neck, hoping she might wake early from her annoying slumber. As I stared at her, I continued counting down each second that her eyes did not open, anticipating the moment when Father would allow me to remove the shield of fabric obscuring her view. Fixated on her unknowing rest, I wished more than anything that I could take her seat, for I longed to know what it was like to be thrust into the horror that surrounded her. Ill-treated all her life, she was about to hit another calamitous jackpot of shit. And this time *my* hands would be liable. Without her lucid company, I was left alone with my thoughts and carried away by the shadow's whispers.

At the precise moment I hit the peak of my most desolate silence, I noticed the slightest bit of movement from her knuckles. As quickly as the snap of one's fingers, she was awake. It elated me that the moment I had waited what seemed like centuries for was about to begin. Yawns emerged from her waking mouth. Rustling movements ensued, and in a prodigious attempt, she tried to free each of her limbs, one by one. During her unsuccessful escape attempt, she rubbed her wrists and ankles raw by bestowing all her force upon the rope. I made my way like a panther around the table to her seat to comfort her. Although she continued to wiggle like a fish meeting dry land, I untied the multiple layers of knots that made her vision impaired. Releasing the shield from her eyes, I patiently waited behind her, for I knew her pupils were still adjusting to the room's lighting. Do not fret about her; being a gentleman, I evaluated my blindfolding strategy to assure she lived a humane life until the ceremonial start. I denounce responsibility for all actions against her from this moment forward, as they are all Father's bidding and not mine.

After several minutes of struggling to rid herself of the restraints, she grew sluggish with exhaustion. It was unmistakable that her vision was regaining clarity; the timing was impeccable. I reclaimed my seat across from her to provide a familiar, lively face to welcome her unblurred gaze. Taking advantage of the last few moments before her eyes gained complete lucidity, I admired the once-empty table now brimming with my family members' faces. Everyone had touched my life and seeing them seated in unity granted me the extraordinary opportunity to both admire and replay each of their unique endings in my head. A warm exhalation of air whisked across my bare neck; conscious of Father's presence, I glanced behind my chair to regard him taking comfort on his throne in the dark corner. His restless manner clarified that he was thirsty for the show to begin. With each tedious moment that passed, his impatience grew. Embracing Father's contentious thoughts, I turned around and glared across the table, where I met Hope's ghostly, wide-open eyes. She was apperceptive, I, delighted. To quell the gaze of bewilderment plastered on her face, I met her stare with the warmest of smiles and a flirtatious wave made by my wiggling fingers. Through her squinting eye slits, I saw confusion amplify on her face as she attempted to process my curious mannerisms. She shifted her gaze from my face to each one that surrounded her, her expression of confusion turned into one of horror. If not for her previous state of complete unconsciousness, which had left her vocal cords rusty, she would have shrieked in terror. Father had forewarned me about her awakening to better protect my listening ears. And he had encouraged my next actions to take flight.

Witnessing the horror fill her eyes, I leaped from my seat, jumping higher than I ever had. I jumped with the joy of a thousand men because I had a real audience of listening ears for once in my life and planned to give my best performance ever. Standing in front of my captive audience, I found myself facing a minor predicament, for I didn't know where to begin my monologue. To arouse my guests' attention, I paced across the front of the body-filled room. I continued my stern stroll until my eyesight caught the enchantment of the dancing glow emanating from the marvelous chandelier, the ornate fixture's treelike appearance comforting me. Awestruck, I found myself transported to memories of riding my steed to and from the Bonnet estate and being met each time by the mysterious willow tree. Whenever I passed the woodsy creature, fascination overtook my body. The tree's lovely siren call elicited immediate pause, allowing me the occasion to admire the beautiful solitude of each of its branches.

Powerful imagery recapitulated in my mind, and a heroic image of the rope tightening around my neck and my dangling limbs swaying in the wind filled my entire being with orgasmic sensations. The anticipation of my body's oxygen being limited sent euphoric quivering through my lungs so intense that it sparked my attention back to the room I was standing in. Upon my mind's arrival, I drew my eyes to the chair in the dark corner; intrigued, I peered closer. Compulsive fixation on the solitary seat converted to fascination as I noticed an unfamiliar object positioned on the cushion. "The shadow must have left me a gift!" I exclaimed with the utmost glee. As I studied the item more intently, I noticed it was a woven cord that bore a striking resemblance to the one from my dreams. The coincidence created a short-lived reemergence of heroic feelings that were purged from my veins by waves of confusion. My mind craved answers to the multitude of questions that flooded my consciousness. Should I seize the rope, and if so, what should I do with the beautiful twine? Was I to wrap it around Hope's frail neck and hang her? Shifting my attention from the rope, I turned toward Hope, who sat attentively in her chair. The rousing image of the rope bound around her fragile skin made prickles creep down my spine. She didn't move or make a sound; in fact, she was so still that her entire body suffered from tetany-like paralysis, except for her eyes, which showed life through the rivers of tears streaming down her face.

"Who's afraid of the Big Bad Wolf?" I asked her with a malicious grin spanning cheek to cheek. I then made my way toward her. Without warning, my casual stroll turned into a sprint, propelling me to approach her seat. After stopping mere inches from Hope's chair, I lowered my body to the floor in a spiderlike crouch and, smelling her fear, leaned toward her ear, and screamed, "*Who's afraid of the Big Bad Wolf?*" She couldn't help but flinch in her seat as fear of the unknown rushed over her face. Her skin turned stark white as it flushed every ounce of color in coordination with the growing desperation in her eyes. Her expression gave assurance that I had her where I wanted her. Overtaken with a sudden sense of spontaneity, I jumped to my feet and galloped over to the chair where Father sat with the mysterious rope. Greeting his dark figure, I collected the rope from his hand and took a seat on his untouchable throne. "Voila, I am the wolf! I am Father!" I proclaimed with a maniacal look in my wide eyes. "I am the predator that wreaks havoc at night, serving both girls and boys a hell of a fright," I serenaded in a whimsical tune to ensure that the words lodged in Hope's memory. Upon hearing the clever melody, she shuddered with fear; her tremble caused my eyes to shimmer with the iridescence of a glorious sunset.

Sitting in Father's chair provided me a clear vision of what was to come of the night, and the insight made my blood curdle with deep anticipation. In that pivotal moment, I slung the rope over my left shoulder as if modeling a fashionable scarf. After making a swift return to my original seat at the dinner table, I sat down and nonchalantly crossed my arms. "Dear Mr. Bonnet, could you pass me the wine?" I said sarcastically, before bursting into uncontrollable laughter at his useless response. Moving my conversation on to the next guest, I turned my chin to the right, where my eyes met the mangled face of the leather-skinned housemaid. "What about you, old hag? Can *you* pass me the wine?" I guffawed; my words barely decipherable as rolling laughter lifted my body from the chair. Though consumed with hysterics, I took a moment from my revelry to enjoy a glance at Hope's face as she attempted to hold back her tears. Immersed in the wave of energy streaming through the room, I sprang to my feet and leaped up to a standing position on my seat cushion, towering over everyone at the table. Now I was assured of having their undivided attention.

Like a tremendous Shakespeare-style sonnet, I unleashed dramatic verses as I theatrically climbed across the dinner table on all fours. As I clambered past each guest, I tossed grapes into their gaping mouths, pausing only to break the plates in front of them. At last, I reached Hope's fear-saturated face. Her emotional demise entertained my guests as it brought out my best comedic abilities. Hearing the audience laud my outstanding performance, I believed an encore was in order. I extended my moist tongue toward her in one fluid motion and licked her face from her chin to her scalp. "Are you afraid of the Big Bad Wolf now?" I asked as I let out a loud chortle in her ear. Not receiving the validation I was expecting, I changed my posture from all fours to an upright position at the edge of the table. Feeling more potent than ever, I looked down upon each peasant and viciously kicked their lifeless heads. "*Do you want to see a show?*" I shouted so forcefully that the veins on my forehead leaped from my skin and spittle spewed from my lips. I then reached for the pocket behind my left lapel and ripped the enshrined paper from its hiding spot. Once I had the token in front of me, I salivated at the sight of my sweet Grace's red lips and licked every drop of blood from the papyrus. Not finding adequate gratification in the deed, I tore the imprinted lips off the folded sheet of paper, tossed them into my mouth, and swallowed the crimson treasure. When I finished, I ostentatiously stuck out my tongue for all to see the skill at which I'd performed the disappearing trick.

I glanced down the length of the table, taking a moment to engage in the praise imparted by each audience member. Each of their faces exhibited renewed excitement in their opened eyes, and their hands expressed pleasure through roaring applause. Father was right; they loved me. "Tighten the beast to be granted the feast," I heard whispered from the dark corner behind me. Distracted by the words, I refocused my attention on the effulgent feature that rested above my head, the beautiful chandelier. Again, I gazed up at its golden trunk and branches. With each deepened glance, I became lost in the sculpted metal. A second whisper pervaded the air behind me, but this time the tone was unfamiliar to my ears. I rotated toward the unknown voice that beckoned me from the murky corner; upon the completion of my pivot, my body froze, surprised by an unexpected jerk of my neck followed by a sense of asphyxiation. As I reoriented myself amid the strangling sensation, I realized that a noose had been placed around my neck. In a panic, I reflected on my earlier path from the chandelier, tracing my steps to determine how I had gotten to this point. Looking above me, I noticed the other end of the rope was secured to the fixture's golden branches. Engulfed by the severity of my situation, I directed my attention back to the shadow for help and felt a warm blanket wrap around me. I had become my dream, and at this moment, I stood facing the world as the most heroic creature in the room. I was even more courageous than Father.

I maneuvered my body to face Hope, who appeared lost in her thoughts, the same expression pervading her eyes as I'd had when the shadow had liberated me from the pitiless streets. She was me and I was she. Mesmerized by the revelation, I took an entranced step toward her, extending my hand to touch her changing image, realizing I had walked off the edge of the carved oak table. The spellbound advance was metamorphic. The moment my feet denounced the secured platform, I heard the familiar deep voice more distinctly than ever: *I'm proud of you, son.* Each comforting word resonated in the deepest depths of my being. The voice continued to soothe me as my neck fractured and my feet dangled. With every inch of suffocation that my body tried to fight, Father wrapped his arms around my soul, sharing warm feelings of sincere devotion with me. In the last moments leading up to my slumber, I knew I had completed everything Father had asked of me. At last, I was going home.

I had sealed each window shut, locked every door, and swallowed the one and only key. The window's glass was double the standard density, making it impossible to break, and the airtight seals created a tomblike effect that imprisoned all sounds within the estate's walls. The only thing witnessed by the distant neighbors would be silence. If, by some wondrous stroke of luck, Hope found a way out of this prison, where would she go? Who did she have left to turn to for help? She had no one! Hope had no hope! I had spared her for a distinct purpose, and if she acquiesced, she would flourish. If she repudiated Father's summons, however, she would forgo his protection, and as the only living being in this house--and a female with known peculiarities--she would indeed be incriminated for every heinous act performed in this godforsaken place. In my hidden pocket where Grace's kiss once lived, now dwells a letter detailing my birth name, lineage, and the story I just disclosed to you. The pocket under the opposite lapel conceals a message addressed to the only living soul who witnessed my last breath, Hope. From the first moment our gaze connected through the distant windowpane, I found her noteworthy. Her disposition and tendencies incited comfort, as they were familiar to my own. The shadow assured me that I was not unbalanced and that many others were just like me. I couldn't help wondering what would happen to her. Would she choose Father's altruistic benevolence or persecution? Would she embrace the calling to save a world that seemed incapable of absolution? Maybe I am wrong to ask the questions, but I can attest that curiosity still follows one to the grave.

Although I am not perfect, I am above the animals of class. I will be their great savior or the greatest fear that haunts them every night until they succumb to their deliverance. I am the dark owl born of no soul. With confidence, I pulled my phantom handkerchief from my pocket to smell my victory. As the stench hit my nose, I looked into the eyes of the dark cobblestone way that lay lifeless under my feet. We are home.

I am Daniel Manly, and she is Hope Bonnet.

Thirteen

THE FINAL FAREWELL

To whoever discovers my dangling corpse:

As we announced our last goodbye, I hoped a tear crept from your roving eye, and if a droplet did not fall, I would not be sad, for I realize my thoughts were quite mad. My mind's wondrous imaginings are rough to any boorish psyche. Though my rebuke might last for many distant years, let me state that I am not the darkened soul you have determined me to be. I was not born into this world as a typical child portrayed in literature. From the moment I laid my eyes on earth's wondrous fascinations, I was different, and I found my happiness a challenge to cultivate. I thought it inconceivable to live another day after my mother began her staggering ill-fated descent down the filth besmirched street at poverty's end. I will not tell you her born name in this part of my reflection, for I want to keep it soaked in formaldehyde, preserving her glory days as she lived them and ended them, with the societal shovel that buried her alive. Just like me, her mother brought her into this life as a bastard child and supplied her the free will to choose various paths. Regardless of how dire the circumstances, we all have choices, and as you will soon see, her decisions were obtuse. She succumbed to a life of hardships by embarking on a harrowing journey as a streetwalking whore. The lifestyle did not treat her with kindness, as evidenced by the vast holes in the base of her pockets, which were incapable of holding a single shilling.

As she was void of a dowry to secure a suitor, her mother forced her into a pernicious life, taking any measure necessary to elevate her impoverished societal position. Her hair was coal-black, matching a raven's feather, and spiraled down her back in ringleted curls that flowed like cascading waterfalls. Each free-flowing tendril grazed her protruding vertebrae and caromed with every step. She was a beautiful bird trapped in an abhorrent cage, cognizant of the horrors that awaited her each day upon the cage's door opening. The tortured woman's single wish was that of comforting warmth, yet she knew life would never choose her for such consolation. Afflicted by societal expectations, she eliminated every fundamental facet of her life to afford materialistic items, thinking each shiny object would lure a wealthy suitor. Her childhood ideals of finding true love were no longer a qualification for a marital match; instead, status and wealth guided her choice. Her considerable financial investment in exotic petticoats left her without food to feed her perfectly shaped mouth. Though most would consider her situation somber, she found it held a silver lining, for her withering frame permitted her to easily cinch her waist to the size of a small orange. Creating the ideal silhouette of the period allowed her to catch the roaming eye of a local duke's son.

Whenever he craved a change of scenery, he forewent his expensive London flat to journey to the nearby town where she lived. Within moments of his arrival, he'd stroll to her location and wait for her to pass by. Each day, like clockwork, she'd saunter down the cobblestone street at half past two. He'd take her friendly singular wave as a signal to follow, always staying a mere ten steps behind her as she continued her daily parade. After several weeks of the same seductive lark, his patience wore thin, and he found her routine a bore. To appease his obsessive carnal appetite, he broadened his scope to encompass stalking her morning patterns. As expected from an individual of altitudinous wealth, his boredom outgrew him, and with his dark sense of entitlement, he consumed her last remaining independent moments, her evening strolls. In society, wealthy men are held in high regard and by default labeled "trustworthy." This societal characterization provides the perfect facade to conceal the vile intent of affluent men void of moral conscience. The duke's son's perfect bone structure and six-foot-tall, lean, muscular frame further cloaked his sinister nature. His dominant presence overtook everyone around him, and his masculine gait made all aware of his impending arrival. Although he and I were akin in the sense that we captured attention from any fair maiden of our choosing, our desires differed. The duke's son craved the filthy streets forbidden fruit, thirsting only for the raven-haired woman. Both day and night, with obsessive infatuation, he stalked the naive woman whose frame continued to disintegrate. He examined her from afar, desperate to glean information about her existence, but her indecipherable facial expression provided him no help in exposing her life story. Though her position in life was unfavorable, my mother still maintained high aspirations for marriage but recognized that the duke's son was beyond her societal reach. She never wasted even the slightest amount of energy entertaining the thought of attracting him as a suitor, knowing she had no chance at a long-term commitment.

After months of studying her daily patterns and private evening routines, the young man plotted his seedy alley surprise. Though at first thrilling, the game of lion and prey lost its excitement once the nefarious suitor broke my mother's seal. He had stolen the only substantive item of value she owned, not giving her a single opportunity to state her objection. After the dreadful event in the alley occurred, the wind held still with mournful sorrow. The thin thread that tied my mother's fragile soul to her being snapped, dragging the life from her weary eyes as it exited her shattered psyche. Void of a soul, the emaciated woman was nothing more than an uninhabited ghostlike shell with pupils that fostered flames of scorched optimism. Within three weeks, she found herself with child, alone in the streets. Duplicitous desperation filled her entire being.

After that night's desecration, the narcissistic childlike man had no intention of returning to the meaningless town, but that changed when he became drunk four months later. Now that you have witnessed the narrative's history, it should ease all feelings of shock when you learn what happens next between the predator and prey. Once the duke's son arrived back at his sordid playground, he was not at all amused by the news that his next of kin was brewing between the legs of his lascivious sacrifice. She tucked away her idealistic speculations regarding the impetus of his grand return to the confines of her rib cage, and for a moment, she was convinced God himself had shepherded him back to extricate them from their dire circumstances. From the monstrous experience that speared through her nonexistent dreams, she surmised a silver lining. Just shy of being four months pregnant, the peasant believed the duke's son would answer her prayers.

The second night after his arrival, he once again followed the unattended expectant mother into the darkened alley. The ground was saturated beyond its capacity, creating lingering pools of precipitation from the rainstorm the night before. Each step by the hunter and hunted over the wet cobblestones created splashing sounds that paralleled drowning ambitions. As their distance tightened, the dreadful noise of hazy footsteps assaulted my mother's ears. The sound triggered remembrances of the alley's nightmare, causing survival instincts to take hold of her body and limbs. Taking a deep breath, she flung her body around to face the ominous creature. Apprehensive relief flooded over her as she realized the behemoth was none other than the duke's son. Now standing face-to-face with him, she observed as his eyes fixated on her growing belly, slogged their way up to her cleavage, and after several lingering moments, stopped at her dirt-stained face. With harsh vocal expressions, his vile mouth clarified that he no longer found her appealing. Ignoring his profanity-filled berating, she saw that moment as her only opportunity for salvation. She buckled to her knees with her pregnant stomach and groveled at his polished shoes. Every lamenting word that tumbled from her lips leapt off her tongue in a tone one might liken to the sound of soft wind chimes. The duke's son stood over her expressionless, listening as she beckoned to his heartstrings and begged him not to forsake her and his child. After her mouth closed for the last time, the dark devil took off a single glove and held out his palm to help her back to her shoeless feet. As she took his hand, she let out a sigh of relief, believing his gesture to be a positive affirmation, when, in fact, he had only removed his-stark white glove to ensure that her muddied hand left no traceable evidence upon him.

Once she was on her feet, his repugnant breath brought news to her ears that struck her core like an ax fracturing firewood. The ruinous words that he was engaged to another of equal societal worth rolled off his forked tongue. To assure that every ounce of hope drained from her frail frame, he added that he no longer had use for a sinful whore. Each harsh word lacerated her eardrums and made her eyes hemorrhage tears at the rate of a severed artery. With one last desperate attempt at physical connection, she reached for his tailcoat, and without reciprocation, he coldheartedly turned his back and bade her farewell. The loss of the wealthy man was devastating, and that harsh reality eradicated every reason to live from her shallow being. One would think the child would be reason enough to exist, but in her eyes its only value was for leverage, and without the man, it served no useful purpose. Many times, she endeavored to rid herself of the fetus but failed, just like everything else she had attempted in her lifetime. Embittered by her unfavorable circumstances, she walked the streets with a defecating gaze until my birth, loathing every minute the child occupied her fetid womb. Bystanders added to her disdain through their gawks and whispers, promulgating her disgraceful state and mental instability. Society had turned against her, a penniless whore who had tried to elevate her status. Even brothel workers had held higher esteem than she did.

When the day came for my arrival, she wasn't there to nurture me or provide anything resembling motherly affection; in fact, she couldn't rid herself of me fast enough, just as society had done to her. After my arrival, she mercilessly left me in the freezing weather on the doorstep of an orphanage. Upon her departure, she was forgotten, never to be heard from again. The shadow once told me she had gone off into the woods to die, but I am unsure whether that is the truth or Father only made it up to protect me. Regardless, she had proven to be of value for birthing the man ordained to conduct the most significant societal reformation in history, and for that contribution, I have pocketed her existence deep in the pit of my stomach. Her story will always cause my blood to boil and fuel my deep loathing for societal standards. Our unfavorable lineage destined us both for a life of misery in this godforsaken world. With each palpitation of my beating heart, I had fought to correct the world's wrongs through my deliberate execution of justice. I lived my life knowing her death, and any that stemmed from my hands, were not in vain. I take the blame for her demise, however, since my birth incited her desire for death. She was indeed my first kill.

Every being has a life force that grows each day they choose to flourish. As a reminder of this notion, I often raised my right hand to the sky, then positioned it across my beating heart, to show my appreciation that there is more to life than miserable treachery. Not only is there more, but what is to come exceeds human comprehension. You might believe me mad, and you may or may not be wrong. But how should you determine me to be more crazed than those who live next door to you? Are stones only cast at me because my ideas do not conform to those constructed with standard bricks by a handful of societal elitists? What if I am the only one who has been provided enlightenment by a higher being trying to help humanity reach eternal paradise? If possessing a nonconforming opinion marks me as insane, so be it. I shall sleep with sweet dreams, knowing I am not a coward for standing by my unconventional ideologies. Your sleep, however, will be wrought with nightmares of indecision because of your unwillingness to embrace free will. You might think me mad, but just wait--you shall soon see the best is yet to come. I will always be with you.

Sincerely,

Daniel Manley

About Author

GITTE TAMAR

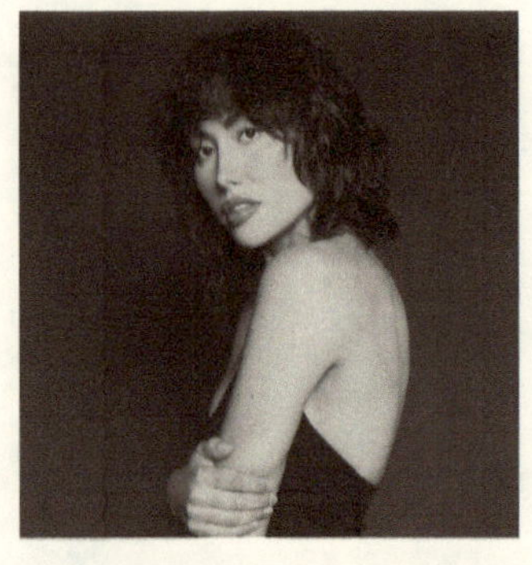 Brigitte, "Gitte", Tamar was born in a small rural Oregon town. Growing up, she was enthralled by scary tales featuring poetic tones and consistently gravitated towards writing darkened narratives. In Shadows That Speak, Brigitte explores the stigma of mental illness in the format of a psychological thriller. *Shadows That Speak* is Brigitte's first commercial horror novel.

www.ingramcontent.com/pod-product-compliance
Lightning Source LLC
Chambersburg PA
CBHW020024310726
48970CB00007B/2186